#29

FALLING IN LOVE

ANN E. STEINKE

SCHOLASTIC INC.
New York Toronto London Auckland Sydney

No part of this publication may be reproduced in whole or in part, or stored in a retrieval system, or transmitted in any form or by any means, electronic, mechanical, photocopying, recording, or otherwise, without written permission of the publisher. For information regarding permission, write to Scholastic Inc., 730 Broadway, New York, NY 10003.

ISBN 0-590-40634-5

12 11 10 9 8 7 6 5 4 3 2 1   7 8 9/8 0 1 2/9

Printed in the U.S.A.   01

First Scholastic printing, May 1987

FALLING IN LOVE

CHEERLEADERS

CHAPTER

Olivia Evans, the captain of the Tarenton High Varsity Cheerleading Squad, had never felt better, had never performed with as much confidence or breathtaking skill. If there's anything to this biorhythm stuff, she thought, preparing for a particularly awe-inspiring jump, then mine are at an all-time high. She took a deep breath and catapulted herself off the minitramp at the side of the gym and went flying through the air to land on Peter Rayman's shoulders. Just as Peter took a step backward, she went into a pike fall and was caught in his arms. Then he tossed her lightly and she fell to the floor, landing in a split. It looked like she should be experiencing excruciating pain, landing like that. But Olivia Evans was an expert at landing in splits; she did them painlessly — and flawlessly.

The cheer ended and both sides of the gym,

1

Tarenton and Deep River fans alike, applauded the tiny, lithe cheerleader who never failed to take their breath away.

Grinning, proud, and pleased, the four girls and two guys of the Varsity Cheerleading Squad ran to the side of the gym as the two teams came back from their halftime break.

Olivia knew that David Duffy, her boyfriend and former student at Deep River High School, was up on the Tarenton side of the gym, probably still feeling somewhat like a traitor even though he now attended college. She glanced up to the spot where she knew he'd be, three rows up and directly behind where the squad sat — when they did sit, which was rarely.

She frowned. Instead of the one-dimple grin of approval which David always bestowed on her when she'd been particularly spectacular, she received no acknowledgement from him at all. He wasn't even looking in the direction of the floor where play had begun.

Craning her neck to see better, Olivia discovered the reason, and her frown deepened. Some girl she didn't recognize was talking animatedly to Duffy. Every other word seemed to be accented by a jab in the air with the pencil she held in her right hand. Then she said something that made David laugh.

Who *was* she? Olivia wondered. And what could they possibly be talking about so intensely that David had missed Olivia's big finale?

"Olivia, don't you think we ought to be cheering Alex? He just got fouled and is going to take a free throw." Tara Armstrong's voice intruded on Olivia's thoughts.

Olivia whipped around guiltily, saw Alex Converse preparing to take his shot, and bounded to her feet.

"Let's hear it for Alex!" she screamed.

The other five joined her in a loose, easy string along the sidelines, cheering Tarenton's finest.

> "Go, Alex, go!
> Make that throw!
> Don't be a stinker,
> Make it a sinker!"

Fortunately for Alex, he made the shot easily.

"I can't stand that cheer," Peter Rayman muttered to Hope Chang. "If the poor sap misses, he gets called a stinker by implication."

"Maybe we should suggest a change to Mrs. Engborg," Hope said, referring to the cheerleaders' coach. She agreed with Peter. It wasn't a particularly flattering cheer for anyone who missed the basket. "But what else rhymes with sinker?"

Peter opened his mouth to answer and stood there gaping. "I can't think of a thing," he finally admitted, running his fingers through his sandy-colored hair. The two of them, who had been dating for months, grinned at each other, then looked back out at the action on the court.

Deep River had the ball and, from the looks

3

of concentration on the Killers' faces, they had no intention of yielding the court to the Tarenton Wolves.

Someone scored for the Killers, and their cheerleaders sprang into action.

"Oooh!" Tara moaned and dropped to the bench for a rest. She hung her head, and masses of red hair cascaded around her face.

The others joined her; Hope and Peter sitting side by side. Peter took Hope's hand and held it.

Suddenly it dawned on him that he hadn't even thought about it. He'd just naturally taken her hand and hadn't even been aware that he'd done it. Had things between them become so routine that touching Hope was unconscious? Wasn't he supposed to be excited by it instead of mildly bored?

Hope was vaguely aware that one of her hands wasn't free, and she looked down in surprise to find it in one of Peter's. How had that happened? Why hadn't she noticed? We're like an old married couple, she thought, her brow puckering slightly; we're doing things by habit instead of intent. Is that the way a seventeen-year-old and a sixteen-year-old's romance should be? Are we supposed to be in a rut already?

Jessica Bennett, a tall, graceful brunette with sparkling green eyes, danced sideways in excitement and glanced quickly behind her. Her gaze locked with Patrick Henley's — just as she'd known it would. Even though he'd graduated

4

the year before, he still attended games. He claimed watching her cheer gave him added incentive.

She smiled widely at him, then puckered up and blew him a kiss. He was such a hunk! And so wonderfully aware of it. He had looks; an incredible physique; and a great, unselfish personality.

She hugged herself in pleasure. Life was perfect. Well, almost, she amended. Life with Patrick was perfect. Life at home was another matter. But she refused to dwell on that. Instead, she would concentrate on cheering the Wolves to victory, then joining the other Varsity Cheerleaders in a celebration afterward with Patrick close by her side. Right where she wanted him!

Patrick gazed lovingly down at the back of Jessica's head. His gaze followed the slope of her shoulders under the white cheerleading sweater, down to the red and white miniskirt. Suddenly she bounded to her feet. The girl was nothing short of outstanding! He still felt the urge to shake himself to make sure he wasn't in some kind of dream and that he and Jessica were really a couple. With his record of falling for girls like Mary Ellen Kirkwood, who loved him but left him, he sometimes wondered if he was kidding himself. But he and Jessica had finally ironed out their troubles. Jessica had stopped being panicked by a permanent relationship with a guy, and he — Patrick Henley, furniture mover and garbage collector extraordinaire — was the guy Jessica cared about.

A silly, lopsided, half-sexy smile spread across his face as he gazed at Jessica.

Sean Dubrow, the other male Varsity Cheerleader, jumped to his feet and stood beside Jessica. There was an intense grudge match being played out on the court between the two teams. Tarenton's star forward, Ray Elliott, was dribbling the ball, alternately trying to sink the basket or pass it to a teammate so he could score. But the Deep River forward was all over him, long arms blocking, fast feet dancing to and fro, preventing Ray from doing anything.

"Come on, ref, call a foul," Sean muttered. "The guy's practically giving Ray mouth-to-mouth, he's so close."

"This is ridiculous," Jessica agreed. "If that guy stood any closer, they'd be wearing the same jersey!" She balled her hands into fists, tense with excitement and anxious for something to break.

Suddenly Ray feinted to the left, then zigzagged to the right, losing his gluelike opponent. He dribbled fast and furiously through the startled players to slam-dunk the ball.

"Y-e-a-h!" Sean crowed, punching the air with one fist.

Tarenton fans sprang to their feet, a cry rising from them that deafened the Varsity Cheerleaders, as they ranged out along the sideline to cheer.

"What a way to go!
We've got 'em on the run!

6

Sink that basket now,
And the game is done!

Which wasn't strictly true. There were six minutes remaining, but the cheer was designed to demoralize their opponents and make them lose heart. *If* they could hear the cheerleaders.

"We'd better use the megaphones," Sean remarked to Olivia as they stood beside each other, watching the game continue with Deep River in possession of the ball.

Olivia spun in place to grab up her megaphone. Her gaze wandered three rows up into the stands and she saw that the strange girl and David were still talking with their heads close together. Obviously the game wasn't interfering with their important conversation, she thought sourly. *Who was that girl?*

She was so preoccupied with Duffy's mystery companion, Olivia missed cuing her squad to cheer for their team, and the Deep River Cheerleaders took over the limelight by forming a chorus-girl-type line to cheer for their team. Fortunately, their performance lacked a lot of conviction.

Sean stood there, hands in the pockets of his red slacks, rocking on the balls of his feet. He was feeling good. It didn't matter what Deep River did now; Tarenton was whipping Deep River 78–49. Awesome! There'd be a celebration and a half with the squad tonight, along with Patrick and Duffy, as usual. But who would he have? Sean frowned. Then his handsome face cleared. If his hands had been free, he'd have snapped his fingers. Deborah Brown, that cute little junior who was in his chemistry class. They were recently paired by their teacher as lab partners, and Sean didn't think he'd imagined her interest in him. And she seemed like a nice, easygoing girl. Earlier in the year Sean had had an ill-fated romance with a girl from Garrison, and had he ever been burned! Then there was that girl in New Orleans, too far away. Romance wasn't his strong point lately, he thought wryly. So maybe he ought to ask someone like Debby out. How could she possibly cause him any trouble?

He looked up into the crowd, spotted Debby sitting in the stands on the left, marked the place mentally, and plotted moving in on her as soon as the game ended. Yes, indeed, little Debby, get your party hat on, 'cuz old Sean Dubrow is taking you out tonight, he thought with a grin.

He returned his attention to the game, and the self-satisfied grin on his face widened joyously as Tarenton stole the ball from Deep River and scored.

The fans grew almost uncontrollable on the Tarenton side of the gym.

"Come on, guys, let's do the 'Running Scared' cheer," Olivia yelled and raced out onto the court as the refs called time out to confer over a difference of opinion about whether Tarenton had committed any foul during that maneuver.

The six formed a staggered line, with Sean and Peter just behind the four girls and between Jessica and Tara, and Hope and Olivia. They stamped their feet and clapped their hands four times as they chanted:

> "Running scared
> Outta control!
> Their team has lost,
> We're on a roll!"

With that, the squad did forward rolls, followed by backward standing tuck jumps. Then they did cartwheels to the right, followed by cartwheels to the left. It was a dizzying cheer but it didn't require a lot of room in which to move, being a semi-sideline cheer. And it was impressive, distracting the rowdy crowd and garnering loud, enthusiastic applause for the squad.

Up in the stands, a pretty blonde girl sat watching the squad. Her beautiful features were marred by a frown. The frown deepened as a boy sitting behind her exclaimed, "Man! Those Varsity girls are something else!"

"Yeah," his friend said, attempting to be clever. "Especially in their cute *short* skirts."

The two freshman boys snickered, making the blonde, Diana Tucker, expel her breath in disgust. When she'd moved from California to Tarenton a couple of months before and had seen how rinkydink it was, she'd known the only way life here would be endurable would be if she belonged to the most popular, "in" group. The most popular group, the one that received the most attention and admiration, and about which all others

9

revolved like spokes of a wheel, was the Varsity Cheerleading Squad. Diana wanted to be a part of that hub in the worst way.

Unfortunately their coach, Ardith Engborg, had told Diana flat out that there wasn't a chance for her to join the squad without 1) her trying out, and 2) a vacancy occurring on the squad. Ardith Engborg had no intention of adding to the number. Maybe next year when Diana was a senior she could try out, the coach had suggested.

Next year! That wasn't soon enough. And Diana was positive her chances of being on the squad next year would be improved one-hundred fold if she were already on the squad *this* year.

So . . . one of those girls had to go. But until now all of Diana's attempts to engineer that had ended in failure.

The two boys behind Diana continued to make juvenile comments on the view afforded them of the cheerleader girls' legs.

Oh, thought Diana, to be down on the floor as a cheerleader instead of having to sit up here in the risers surrounded by little drips like them! She just had to get on the squad. But how? *How?*

CHAPTER

2

The Tarenton fans were chanting, counting down the seconds of play remaining before the game ended.

"Five, four, three, two — "

And with only two seconds remaining, Tarenton's center, Joe Vogel, sent the ball 25 feet through the air and sank it just as the buzzer sounded.

The stands erupted into frenzied activity as fans swarmed down on the court.

The cheerleaders jumped up and down, shouting and hugging each other in ecstasy. Tarenton had creamed Deep River 82–49. It had been a stunning victory!

Olivia's excited gaze swept over the crowd surging down the risers, searching for signs of a tall, cute, blond boy wearing a navy blue yachting cap. But there was none. Where was he? Surely David hadn't left. He wouldn't go out and wait in the lobby for her without telling her, would he? She bit her lip and stood there, her shoulders buffeted by kids pushing past her.

Sean made a beeline for Debby Brown, intent on snagging her before she got out the door.

Patrick came up behind Jessica and swept the unsuspecting girl into his arms. Laughing, she let him bestow a kiss on her cheek in congratulations for a job well-done.

Hope and Peter, without really deciding on it, moved as one out of the gym, heading for the locker rooms.

Tara gabbed with friends, exchanged congratulations, then headed for the locker room, too.

It was only five minutes after the game had ended and the gym was half emptied that Olivia finally spotted David and found out why she hadn't been able to before. He was sitting down — *still* talking to that girl.

Resisting the urge to storm out of the gym, Olivia forced herself to mount the risers toward him, and when she was within talking distance, to inquire sweetly, "David? What's going on?"

He looked up, surprised, then glanced around as if it had just dawned on him that the game was over.

"Oh, Livvy. I'd like you to meet someone from my hometown and *your* rival school tonight."

"Oh?" Olivia's dark gaze shifted toward the girl who sat beside David. She did not like the girl any more closer up than she had when seeing her from a distance. If anything, Olivia liked her even less. She had long, black hair that was braided into one fat plait halfway down her back. Her clothes were a little odd: denim jean jacket, faded jeans, beat-up Indian moccasins, and an old stained sweat shirt under the jacket. She wore little makeup, but Olivia noticed she was stunningly beautiful without it.

"This is Jennifer Clark. She's a senior, and she's taking journalism. Wants to be a sports reporter like yours truly." David gave a mock bow at this and tipped his cap, one of the many hats in his collection. "Jennifer is the star forward on Deep River's girls' basketball team. She's racked up two hundred thirty-one points all by herself so far this season. Jen, meet Olivia Evans, the captain of that superlative cheerleading squad."

"Hello, Olivia," Jennifer said, but she didn't extend her hand or make any other gestures that would convey her pleasure at this meeting.

Olivia nodded curtly, saying, "Hello," just as coolly.

David gave no indication of noticing the lack of enthusiasm between the two. Standing, he explained, "Jennifer spotted me in the stands over here and had to come talk to me. She's read my stuff and wants me to show her the ropes, give her some helpful pointers. I've agreed to take her under my wing so she can get an idea of just what kind of questions are unique to covering sports as opposed to regular news events." His blue eyes crinkled up, and his right cheek dimpled as he quipped, "Makes me feel like the old pro teaching the young upstart."

"Oh, Duffy," Jennifer laughed, using his nickname. She placed a hand on his forearm to help herself to her feet. Once she was standing, though, she kept her hand there, Olivia noted grimly. "That's silly. You're just more experienced than I am. I can learn a *lot f*rom you." She laughed, David grinned, and Olivia fought down the urge to shove Miss Jock off the risers.

"I've invited Jen to come along with us after the game. That way I can give her a ride home afterward and we can talk shop. I hope you don't mind." David's clear blue gaze fastened on Olivia.

The turkey, she thought. He really, honestly, expects me *not* to mind.

"No," Olivia returned virtuously. But she couldn't resist adding, "If she doesn't mind placing herself in jeopardy. After all, she'll be in Wolves territory, surrounded by Tarenton kids."

She aimed a sweetly malicious look at Jennifer, who responded promptly and with equal malice, "Oh, Duffy will protect me. Won't you, fellow news hound?"

Jennifer punched David playfully on the shoulder and he laughed. "Right, us against them. Sounds dangerous but exciting."

"Duffy . . ." Olivia began threateningly. Had she ever set herself up for that!

"Only kidding, honey," he said, planting a conciliatory kiss on Olivia's cheek.

To Olivia's satisfaction, the kiss brought a

narrow-eyed look of disapproval to Jennifer's face.

"Well, then I'll see you later," Olivia said to David, and turned to head back down the risers. She plodded out of the gym toward the locker room. Each footstep that took her away from David and Jennifer felt like doom. She was allowing that black-haired fiend time alone with David, and with foreboding, Olivia knew that was a big mistake. But they'd be spending more time together in the future. Was there any way that Olivia could prevent it? As she shoved the locker room door open and entered the room, Olivia knew the answer. It was no.

The Pizza Palace was crowded with exhilarated kids. As the six cheerleaders, with Patrick, Debby Brown, David, and Jennifer Clark, sat crowded around a large table, people flowed around them, shouting to each other.

Sean had his arm loosely over the back of Debby's chair, and every now and then when he talked, he'd briefly touch her shoulder.

Tara felt vaguely bothered by that. She knew it wasn't because she wished she were in Debby's place. Sean was great, but they never seemed to be able to get serious with each other, probably because they were too much alike. Her dissatisfied feeling was caused by the fact that all the cheerleaders at the table had a special someone: Jessica had Patrick; Hope had Peter, and vice versa; and Olivia had David, although what's-her-name —

from *Deep River*, no less! — seemed intent on getting cozy with David. And Tara? Who did she have? No one. Zilch. What's wrong with me? she wondered, glancing around the room. The boys present seemed to fall into two categories: either 1) boys who were not Tara's type, or 2) boys she'd already dated — not a one worthy of even flirting with.

Then she shook herself. Good grief! she thought. Here I am only just turned 18 and already I've dated so many boys I'm jaded. All the boys I know are b–o–r–i–n–g.

She sighed and took an unenthusiastic bite of her pizza, chewing it without really tasting it. I wish, she thought fervently, that something out of the ordinary would happen to liven things up. If we can get a new girl from California like Diana Tucker to move into town, *why* can't we get a great-looking guy?

Suddenly the very girl she'd briefly thought about appeared at their table — Diana Tucker, on the arm of one of the more valuable players in that night's game, Ray Elliott.

It figures, Tara thought in disgust. She had dated Ray herself, but that was a while back. Diana always seemed to have a knack for getting herself hooked up with the best boys.

"Hello, guys," Diana greeted them. "Great game tonight, huh?"

The cheerleaders, who had come to regard Diana as suspect, returned her greeting with various degrees of enthusiasm, ranging from a minus two (from Tara) to about a four (from

16

Jessica who had, as yet, to have any kind of direct trouble with Diana).

Ray, on whom Diana hung, smiled widely at them all when their attention shifted to him and they praised his contribution to the game.

While the compliments were flowing, Diana's cool blue gaze ranged over the occupants of the table.

Little Olivia, next to David Duffy. And some strange girl next to David. Diana was fairly sure she wasn't from Tarenton. The girl looked ill at ease, although she was masking it pretty well. Diana prided herself on being adept at reading people. The girl kept touching David — on the arm, the shoulder, the back — and sometimes leaning close to make comments. David wasn't exactly telling her to buzz off, either. Hmmm . . . Diana mused.

Her gaze moved on.

Hope and Peter. Two peas in a pod, inseparable. And Peter wouldn't come near Diana now if his life depended on it. One of her failures. Diana grimaced and her blue eyes lit on the next couple in line.

Jessica and Patrick. Just looking at the happy couple made Diana seethe. Talk about wholesome and sweet. Nothing could break *them* apart.

Sean sat next to Jessica, his arm around some girl on his other side whom Diana had seen but didn't know by name. She'd seen her in the halls, but —

Suddenly a thought popped full-blown from the back of her mind. Her attention returned to

Jessica and Patrick. Could she? Would it be possible? Not without a lot of investigation and waiting for the right opportunity. But it wasn't out of the question. Diana's fingers tapped on Ray's arm as she contemplated the feasibility of her plan. Ray thought it was a signal to move on. Fine with me, she thought, her heart lifting at the scheme forming in her mind.

" 'Bye, guys. See you Monday," Diana said, smiling brightly at them all. The couple moved off.

"That's what we're afraid of," Tara muttered under her breath.

Peter, sitting next to her, heard and chuckled. "Got a jack in your car tonight?" he asked, his blue eyes twinkling. He was referring to a time when Tara had been stuck out in the country with a flat tire — and no jack, thanks to Diana's little trick.

Tara laughed, said, "You bet!" and reached for her Coke.

CHAPTER

Fretful mutterings in French were coming from the Armstrong kitchen. They were interspersed with the sound of a congested nose being blown with great vigor. The mutterings rose in volume as Tara entered the kitchen just in time to see Marie, their French housekeeper, yield to a sneezing fit — three in a row.

"Marie!" Tara exclaimed, catching sight of the woman's red-rimmed dark brown eyes. "You're sick!"

Marie, a buxom woman with graying black hair, waved this aside. "*Non*, it is just the little sniffles." All her "i's" sounded like "e's."

"You shouldn't be out here working," Tara commented, reaching to sneak a sample of the canapés Marie had resting on a silver platter beside the stove.

"Ah! And who would prepare all the little delicacies for your parents' grand party tonight?"

Marie sniffed, dabbed at her nose, and plunged into the refrigerator to forage around in the back. Then she exclaimed, *"Non! Non!"* and started rummaging furiously throughout all the drawers and pawing in all the corners. Her exclamations of dismay became more pungent, tipping Tara off to the fact that something was very wrong.

"What's the matter, Marie?" She smiled at the woman's hunched figure. Sometimes Marie could be so harsh-sounding, masking her heart of gold.

More exclamations preceded the slamming of the refrigerator door, and Marie looked wildly around the room. Her hands gestured in agitation as she explained, "Capers! I do not have capers. How can I be expected to cook without capers?" She sneezed, then muttered, "I will have to go out and buy them — "

"No, no, let me," Tara offered instantly. "Now that I have my own wheels I can zip out and get the . . . um . . . capers." She smiled and added, "That is, if you'll tell me what capers *are*."

"That is no problem; they are in the specialty section — you know, the gourmet part. They are small, green, round, somewhat like a berry in shape, and they come in a tall, slim bottle. You will have no problem finding them. The bottle says 'capers.' " Marie smiled widely, looking pleased with her description.

Tara laughed dubiously. Never having bothered even looking in the gourmet section, she had a few doubts about finding these things called capers.

"I'll be right back," she said, turning to run upstairs for her purse and the keys to her "new" gold convertible. Maybe she'd find a handsome grocery store worker to ask for help. She smiled at the prospect.

Outside the house, she settled herself in the driver's seat of her car, carefully arranging the skirt of her dress. Perhaps she should have changed before heading out to the store. She'd been dressed to put in an appearance at the huge party her parents were putting on for some business associates.

She decided there was no time for changing. Who knew how soon Marie needed her capers? She'd better just get them as quickly as possible. Besides, the dress wasn't all that fancy. It looked like something out of the thirties or forties. Gauze georgette in mauve made up the flared slim skirt and the wrapped bodice. Three-quarter push-up sleeves with padded shoulders and a patent leather cinch belt gave her already perfect figure even more of a curvaceous appearance. She knew she looked like dynamite. All the better for impressing boys, she thought with a grin.

Then the grin slipped off her pretty face as she backed out of the driveway. Who was she kidding? No cute boys she knew worked at the grocery store. Sighing, Tara turned at the end of the tree-shaded street. Face it, she thought, all you're going to find at the grocery store are capers.

Olivia counted to three, slowly. Then, speaking even more slowly and carefully, she said into the mouthpiece, "What do you mean, David? Are you breaking our date tonight?" Her voice was oh-so-controlled, but inwardly she was shaking.

"Well, we didn't really have anything definite planned. We were just going to hang around, maybe go to the mall. I didn't think you'd mind. But I have to finish this story and get it in before nine o'clock or it won't make the Sunday morning edition." There was a pause, then Duffy added, "I thought you'd understand. Aren't there times when you have to put in extra practice time for a game and your social life has to take a backseat?"

She knew he was right, but she didn't want to admit it. Besides, he'd had the entire day to write that article. What had prevented him? She didn't want to ask. But the suspicion grew that he hadn't been alone all day. Had he been showing that black-haired news jock the "ropes" all that time?

"Well," she said, since neither of them had spoken in the last thirty seconds, "if that's the way it has to be, so be it. I'll . . . um . . . see you sometime."

David heaved a long sigh, followed by, "Like tomorrow night? I'm not canceling our romance, just our date tonight. What's eating you?"

How like a man, to stab you in the back and then ask why you're in pain. Olivia compressed her lips, took a deep breath through her nose, then said with forced lightness, "Nothing. Don't be silly. I'll see you tomorrow."

How like a woman! David was thinking in exasperation. First they put on the deep-freeze, injured air, then tell you it's all in your imagina-

22

tion. "About five?" he inquired hopefully. "We can get some burgers or something?"

"Sure."

No emotion at all this time. Communication was definitely at its lowest ebb, they both thought.

They hung up, and Olivia brooded at the silent phone for a while. I am not going to press the panic button simply because David is canceling our date — exactly one day after he's agreed to show Jennifer Clark, this world's answer to the female sportswriter shortage, the "ropes"! There may be a few "ropes" I'd like to show her, she thought, grinning at her own malevolence.

She turned and walked down the hall toward the kitchen, where she knew her mother was working on dinner and expected her help. The last thing she felt like doing was eating. But if she had a fight on her hands, she might as well be well-fortified, she thought a little grimly.

"Capers . . . capers . . . capers . . ." Tara was muttering to herself. Except for her having no accent, she sounded like Marie rambling on under her breath. There! They were right down on the second from the bottom shelf. Bending over, Tara reached for the slim green bottle — and suddenly she was sent staggering! Flailing her arms, Tara grabbed the edge of the store shelf for support. Someone had hit her with a shopping cart, right when she'd been bent over! How embarrassing!

Slowly, fuming every second, she turned to give the person a piece of her mind.

And stood there gaping!

23

Standing before her, with a face and neck the color of her mother's prized red roses, was one of the most gorgeous guys she'd ever seen.

"I'm so sorry! I . . . uh . . . I'm just, well, I wasn't looking because I don't know this store and I guess I just got involved in trying to read all the signs for the aisles overhead and . . . um. . . ." His deep, distressed voice trailed off and he stood there, gazing at her helplessly with incredible blue eyes.

"Oh, that's okay. Don't worry about it. I know what you mean. I don't come here a lot, either." Tara looked back at the hunk, thinking how different her reaction was to the one she would have had if it had been some ordinary person standing there instead of this blond, muscular specimen of masculinity. Oh, he was too gorgeous to believe! And Tara was positive she'd never seen him in her life. If she had, she would have remembered.

"Are you all right?" he asked, looking, if possible, even more uncomfortable than before.

Tara, resisting the urge to rub the sore spot, said, "Oh, sure, I'm just fine."

They gazed at each other for a long moment, during which Tara knew he was giving her the once-over just as surreptitiously as she was him.

Tara guessed his age to be around twenty. He was probably about six feet tall. All in all, the guy was someone worth knowing, and Tara didn't waste any time.

"Did you say you didn't know this store? Are you new in town?" She gazed at him directly, her

24

dark eyes letting him know she was interested.

"Yeah. I just moved into an apartment last night. I don't know where anything is." He grinned easily, obviously relieved by Tara's friendly attitude in spite of the fact that he'd literally run into her. "Especially in this store. Can't find a thing." He shrugged in an appealing way.

Tara was quick to seize the opportunity. "Tell me what you need to know. I've lived in this little town all my life, and if I don't know where a place is, it doesn't exist." She smiled encouragingly at him, stepping closer. The capers were forgotten for the moment. Number one on her agenda was getting as much information about Mr. Gorgeous here as possible.

He smiled, showing even, white teeth. "That would be great. Let's see . . . what do I need to know?" He smiled even wider, shrugging those impressive shoulders. "I need to know *everything*. For starters, where's a great place for pizza?"

"Oh, that's easy. The Pizza Palace. It's the best in town. Now try me with a hard one."

"Ah . . . gasoline — where can I get it free?" He grinned, knowing he was joking.

Tara joined him in the joke, saying smartly, "The Mobil station on Maple Street. *After* hours." They laughed, and Tara added, "Of course, if you get caught I will disavow any knowledge of your activities."

They both grinned and watched as a man with two screaming babies rolled his cart by them. Then when the decibels had died down, he said,

25

"But seriously, where's a good place for breakfast? We bachelors need a hearty meal so we can face the day."

Tara wondered if he'd couched his question in those words deliberately to let her know he was single. Even if it hadn't been on purpose, it was great information.

"The Pancake House on Main Street is probably the best."

"Great."

They stood there, each looking like they wanted to keep talking but not really knowing what to say. Then Tara remembered why she was in the store in the first place and glanced at her watch. "Oops! I have to run. Need to get these — " she paused to reach down to get the green bottle of capers from the shelf " — home so our housekeeper can whip up one of her usual fantastic snacks." Without wanting to, she turned to leave, trying not to look too wistfully at the hunk. "By the way, what's the name of that runaway cart's driver?" She grinned at him, and fluffed her thick red hair around her face.

Returning her grin, he did a short mock bow. "Nick Stewart at your service."

Tara laughed, matching his bow with a small mock curtsy, and said, "Tara Armstrong. Do kindly look where you're driving next time, won't you?"

"Definitely," Nick said with a self-conscious laugh.

It was clear that this was the point where they said good-bye, but it was also clear that neither of them was ready to do it. But it was imperative that Tara get those stupid capers home right away or Marie would be having conniptions.

Sighing a little, she said, "Well, welcome to the town. Perhaps we'll meet again." But when? she wondered as she turned reluctantly away and started down the aisle. Chancing a quick glance back to see what Nick was doing, she was surprised to see he was standing in the same place, staring after her. What was he thinking? Had he been as interested in her as she was in him? Tara hoped so. And she hoped more than anything that somehow, some way, some place, they would run into each other again.

CHAPTER

Jessica paused while raising her fork to her mouth and asked sharply, "What did you just say, Mom?" Normally she managed to make it through dinner in a kind of trance. Usually her stepfather and mother would be engaged in conversations that either excluded Jessica by their content, or were about money. Jessica studiously avoided joining any discussion about money. But somewhere in a corner of her mind not occupied with thoughts of Patrick, she'd managed to hear her mother say a name that even now didn't fail to resurrect old feelings of doubt.

"I said Mary Ellen Kirkwood was in the shop today talking to Mrs. Gunderson right before closing time. I understand she's here for a very brief, unplanned visit. Something about her mother having an operation this week. I'm not sure of all the details, naturally, because I heard all this from one aisle over."

"Oh." Jessica sat there, all appetite lost. How long was Mary Ellen going to be in town? And would she make any effort to see Patrick? It didn't matter how many times he assured Jessica he was all over Mary Ellen now; Jessica still had a hard time believing any red-blooded male could ever completely get over a stunning beauty like Mary Ellen. With a sinking heart, Jessica thought, Especially now that she's a professional model in New York City and really knows how to dress and make up her already flawless features, there is just no way I could ever compete. Sorry as she was that Mrs. Kirkwood needed some kind of operation, Jessica hoped fervently that it would occupy Mary Ellen's time to the point where she was unable to see Patrick this trip.

Call me selfish, she thought with a grimace. I don't care. I just don't want Mary Ellen Kirkwood anywhere within a thousand miles of Patrick Henley. In fact, if he adored her from afar for years, twenty miles just might not be far enough. Make it a million.

Pushing back her chair, she said, "I have a lot of homework that I need to get cracking on, so. . . ." Leaving it at that, she took her plate out to the kitchen, placed it in the dishwasher, and trudged upstairs. Well, she decided as she opened her bedroom door, if Patrick doesn't know Mary Ellen's in town, he won't want to see her. And I, for one, have no intention of telling him.

Olivia Evans stared gloomily out the front

window of her house at the steady drizzle that had been falling the whole afternoon. If Duffy had been free to go out yesterday as planned, she was thinking resentfully, we would have had good weather. But no, he had to cancel, and now look at the great stuff we get to go out in. Her tiny foot tapped impatiently as she waited for his silver car to drive up in front.

Then she had to laugh at herself. She was getting so worked up because a guy had canceled a date and changed it to the next night. Really, she ought to have her head examined. After all, he could have canceled it permanently, not simply changed it. What was the matter with her that she was reacting so emotionally? Unwanted, deep down inside, there was the stirring of an answer, and it was an answer she didn't like to think about.

Turning sharply, she walked over to the chair by the door and grabbed her jacket. Maybe she'd wait outside on the porch for Duffy. That way fresh air — albeit damp fresh air — might blow some sense into her.

"I'm going outside to wait, Mom," she cried and shut the door firmly behind her before she could hear her mother's predictable answer. *Do you think you ought to be out in the damp air? It's still chilly, you know. I think. . . .* On and on she'd go until Olivia would feel like screaming. And she wasn't about to scream. That wasn't a sign of a person in control, and Olivia wanted, above all else, to be in control — of herself and of her life. Mrs. Evans thought the scars, both

30

emotional and physical, that Olivia had supposedly suffered from the heart surgery she'd had as a child gave Mrs. Evans the right to dictate that Olivia live life on the sidelines. Olivia had no intention of doing that. Get right out in the middle of things! That's the way she wanted to live, and so far nothing had stopped her. Not even her mother. *But,* she heard that horrid little voice she'd been trying to muzzle in the house, *could another girl ruin things for you? How much control did you have when Walt wanted to dump you?*

Shivering slightly, she wrapped her jacket closer around her and was intensely glad when she caught sight of David's silver compact car rounding the corner down the street. Running lightly, she made it to the end of the walk before Duffy arrived and opened the door just as he drove up to the curb.

"Hi," she said breathlessly, getting into the car. But before she could say anything more, Duffy started apologizing.

"I'm sorry I'm a little late. But I got involved in showing Jennifer the pressroom down at the *Tarenton Lighter,* and we got into a deep discussion with Hank, the regular sportswriter. . . ." Whatever he said next was drowned out by the roaring in Olivia's head.

The creep! Wasn't seeing Jennifer once a week enough? Did he have to see her once a *day*?

Unavoidably, David's voice intruded on her thoughts.

31

". . . so I bought her lunch and we. . . ."

She was disgusted that she'd nearly lost control, and had resumed listening to his hateful voice — Suddenly she jerked involuntarily. *Hateful?* Was that the kind of adjective she was applying to anything to do with David Duffy now? Hateful. . . . She'd better get a handle on herself or she could lose Duffy! And she didn't want to do that.

"That's all right," she said sweetly, and turned a smiling face to Duffy.

He looked at her as if she were a stranger. Well, he was thinking, maybe she was. After the polar treatment of yesterday, this warm-up was nice, if surprising. How could you ever understand a woman? Jennifer, at least, was a nice, straightforward girl. He liked dealing with her. There was no subterfuge, no putting on an act; just simple, basic, person-to-person interaction without all that boy-girl stuff. It was great. And it was a lot easier to deal with than the mercurial changes Olivia seemed to be going through lately.

Well, maybe today things would go fine. He certainly hoped so. He wasn't in the mood for having to work too hard mentally. That session with Jennifer almost fried his brain. She was so smart, and caught on so quickly. And she had such interesting questions. . . . Suddenly he realized that conversation between himself and his date was nil. Feeling slightly guilty for tuning her out, he glanced at Olivia and saw that she was staring out the windshield with an odd expression. What was she thinking?

This is just great! Olivia thought. Was this the date I wanted so badly? Aren't we having fun? I should demand that the guy take me home right now. It's obvious he's preoccupied and has over-extended himself for the day, what with the tour of the pressroom with Jennifer. What *else* did he do with Ms. Sportswriter? Olivia wondered bitterly. Were there any dark romantic corners at the newspaper office? She wouldn't know; David had never shown *her* the pressroom.

"So where do you want to go?" David asked, watching Olivia carefully for signs of what her mood was like.

She roused herself and looked at him. He seemed to be watching her as if he expected to see her explode any second. Good!

"Oh, anyplace is fine. How about we go to the mall?"

"Sure. Anything the lady wants, she gets." He grinned at her and turned the car around the corner to head for the only mall Tarenton boasted.

I doubt it, Olivia thought dryly.

Blue eyes were narrowed in thought while a hand absently played with a lock of long blonde hair. Hmm . . . Diana was thinking as she watched Patrick Henley pay for his food and head for a booth near the window of the Farm Shop. His tray held a quarter-pound hamburger, a large order of fries, a huge thick shake, and something else Diana couldn't identify.

However, Patrick's large appetite wasn't the prime concern on Diana's mind at the moment.

She had just passed by Marnie's and had happened to see a beautiful woman come out — well not actually a woman, but anyone who didn't know her would have thought so. She was so elegantly dressed and had such a presence about her, she gave the impression of being older. But Diana knew Mary Ellen Kirkwood had only been out of high school less than a year. She didn't know Mary Ellen personally, but what she did know about her was considerable. For one thing, she knew that Mary Ellen and Patrick Henley had had an on-again/off-again romance in school. And there Patrick sat, right here in the very same mall in which Mary Ellen was. Did either of them know that? Smiling wickedly, Diana decided it was only neighborly that she made sure they did.

Turning into the Farm Shop, she approached the counter, bought a diet Coke, and turned, letting her gaze sweep the room as if she were searching for a vacant booth. Then she acted surprised to see Patrick before carefully picking her way through the tables and chairs to his side.

"Well, hello, there! Care to share your booth with a lonesome girl?" She beamed at him in a manner that made it impolite to refuse her.

Stifling a grimace, Patrick nodded at the bench seat opposite him in the booth. "Sure, go ahead." He'd heard tales about Diana Tucker, but never had been on the receiving end of any of her little schemes. He wasn't positive he wanted to have anything to do with her, but at the moment he didn't see how he could get out of it.

Diana wasted no time.

"I was just wandering around the mall, waiting for someone, and I happened to go by Marnie's." She took a moment out to digress and really keep Patrick hanging. "You know, that store that sells the fabulous clothes all the girls at school love? Well, all the girls in *town* love," she amended with a laugh. Then she made an artful start, looking intently at Patrick, and said as if it had just occurred to her, "Oh! And speaking of girls in town. Did you know that Mary Ellen Kirkwood is in town? You know, that girl who was the captain of Varsity Cheerleading last year? In fact, I just saw her right in Marnie's. Which is why I remembered — "

Patrick's reaction was gratifying. He sat bolt upright in his seat and looked out through the window at the passersby as if he expected to spot Mary Ellen himself.

"You did? She is?" He glanced down at his food, apparently considering abandoning it, but then seemed to shrug mentally and take a bite of his hamburger, instead.

Diana needed no further indication that her suspicions were correct. Even if Patrick wasn't leaving his food to leap up and race to Mary Ellen's side, that didn't mean he wasn't still interested in her, despite his supposed involvement with Jessica Bennett. So . . . Diana was just going to have to move into action.

With a quick look at her watch, she exclaimed, "Oh, I'm late for meeting . . . um. . . ." She paused and smiled secretively, as if she were having a rendezvous with some fabulous guy

35

whose identity wasn't to be revealed. "I'd better go. Thanks for sharing your booth with me." She rose and removed herself from the Farm Shop with as much haste as possible without actually running.

CHAPTER

5

Jessica stood in front of Marnie's, gazing at a dress in the front window and knowing, much as she loved it, that she could never have it. Not as long as Daniel controlled the purse strings in the Bennett house. Even though her mother worked hard for her paycheck as a salesperson at Marnie's, Daniel didn't give her carte blanche to spend it as she wanted to. And she wanted to spend some of it on trendy clothes for her daughter, but unfortunately they both knew Daniel would have a stroke. It wasn't that he was a Scrooge; it was just that he felt the mantle of responsibility for the family finances too heavily upon his shoulders.

It was a shame, really, that that luscious dress, all silky and printed in the dreamiest colors, would never grace Jessica's body — at least not in this lifetime. She knew Patrick would love it on her; it was the exact sort of thing he said he liked to see girls wearing. Sighing, Jessica pushed in the door and entered the exclusive shop, searching among the occupants for Mrs. Gunderson, the owner.

The day before, her mother had mistakenly left her extra sweater in the back storeroom where employees placed their things during work hours. Since Jessica had been planning on coming to the mall on Sunday, her mother had appointed her as the retriever of the forgotten garment.

Suddenly Jessica's breath came out in a whoosh as her eyes lit on someone — a familiar someone. *Not* Mrs. Gunderson.

Mary Ellen Kirkwood.

What was with that girl? Why was she in this store so much during her trip home from New York? Why wasn't she with her mother?

Torn between the urge to duck out and the urge to approach Mary Ellen and find out how long she'd be in town, Jessica stood there indecisively until it was too late to do either. Mary Ellen walked briskly out of Marnie's and got lost in the rest of the Sunday afternoon shoppers.

Just as well, Jessica thought. I don't really want to have to be civil to Patrick's old girl friend anyway. Although the way he told it, Mary Ellen had actually been his girlfriend for only a short time; the rest of the time she'd been playing the field — to quite an extent.

Breathing an undeniable sigh of relief, Jessica moved deeper into the store and sought out the owner. At least now she could get her mother's sweater, freed from the fear of seeing Mary Ellen again.

Out in the main part of the mall, Diana Tucker began her trek down the corridor, glancing into each store until finally she spied Mary Ellen. Ambling up to where the beautiful blonde was looking over some lipsticks in the drugstore, Diana pretended to be fascinated by the shades offered.

"Aren't the shades of lipsticks scrumptious this year?" she commented. Then glancing at Mary Ellen as if she'd just realized to whom she was making the apparently idle remark, she exclaimed, "Oh, why, aren't you Mary Ellen Kirkwood? The captain of Varsity Cheerleading last year?"

Mary Ellen looked at her, confused. She didn't recognize this person at all. "Yes, and you. . . ?"

"I'm new this year, but I've seen pictures of you in last year's yearbook, and, of course, people still talk about you, what a fabulous cheerleader you were. . . ."

Mary Ellen smiled warmly, and said, "They *do*?" She could still feel a certain pride whenever people complimented her on the job she'd done as captain of the cheerleading squad last year. There were even still times when she missed it terribly. It all seemed like such a simple existence compared to the life she was leading now.

"Yes, in fact, I was just in the Farm Shop with a boy who was in your class last year, and he couldn't stop talking about you." Diana paused.

"Oh? Who?"

"Why, Patrick Henley. Do you know him?" Diana's blue eyes gazed artlessly at Mary Ellen's.

"Patrick?" Mary Ellen exclaimed in pleasure. "He was in the Farm Shop? Oh, I ought to go see him." She put a lipstick back in the display case and paused before turning away to say, "Nice meeting you, uh. . . ."

"Diana Tucker."

"Diana," Mary Ellen repeated, her mind obviously already on something else. "Thanks. 'Bye."

Mary Ellen left the drugstore at a brisk pace. Good old Patrick. She wanted to see him, to talk over some ideas she had. He had always been a straightforward thinker. He could advise her. And of course, he'd never forgive her if she didn't tell him about her mother.

Diana watched the blonde leave the drugstore, feeling immense satisfaction. Phase One completed. Too bad Jessica Bennett wasn't in the mall today, so she could put Phase Two into action. But Diana would just have to come up with a way to make sure Jessica knew that Mary Ellen was back in town and *seeing* Patrick Henley. That is, if she did. What if Patrick had finished his monstrous snack (It was three in the afternoon, so it couldn't be lunch, could it?) and had left the place in search of Mary Ellen? What if the two of them searched the whole mall and fate, as it sometimes did, played a trick on them and they never actually saw each other? That would be terrible! Diana put down the lipstick she was holding absent-mindedly and raced out of the drugstore, heading

40

for the Farm Shop to see if her plan had hit a snag.

Diana decided things were absolutely perfect. She wished she had a camera for this occasion, but she guessed her word would have to be sufficient.

There they were: Patrick and Mary Ellen. Amazing how good the two names sounded together. Mary Ellen had succeeded in finding Patrick in the Farm Shop, and Diana had succeeded in finding them both together. Perfect!

Smiling in satisfaction, Diana turned and headed down the mall toward an exit. She needed to get home and continue to formulate her plan. It had to be foolproof.

Then, unbelievably, just as she was approaching Marnie's again, who should come out of the store but Jessica Bennett!

"Jessica!" Diana crooned as if greeting her best friend. "How are you?"

The brown-haired girl turned, and her green eyes showed surprise as she said, "Oh, Diana. Hi. I'm fine. And you?"

Silly, meaningless drivel, Diana thought, but necessary for laying the groundwork.

"Exhausted. I . . . um . . . was just thinking of grabbing a cold drink. Shopping is thirsty work," she joked with a laugh.

Jessica smiled and agreed, "Yes, all that money changing hands usually has me hyperventilating, which then has me thirsty."

The two smiled at each other.

"Say, are you here with anybody?" Diana asked, hoping the answer was no.

It was.

"No, I'm just on an errand for my mother."

"Well, then why don't you join me and we'll grab a thirst-quencher at, um, say the Farm Shop. I hear they have some great shakes — or any other kind of drink you could want." She looked at Jessica innocently.

Jessica paused to consider it, then nodded her head, making her shoulder-length brown hair move gracefully. "Sure, why not?" In reality she didn't want to go home, and since nothing else was putting a demand on her time, she might as well try to be friendly to Diana. It couldn't hurt, could it?

They turned toward the Farm Shop. Diana kept up a line of chatter so the unsuspecting girl wouldn't pay much attention to her surroundings. It wouldn't do for her to see what Diana wanted her to see before the absolute perfect moment.

Just five feet from the edge of the first window of the Farm Shop, Diana waved a hand at the restaurant and said, "There it is. And this *must* be the right place. Look who's here already. And get a load of how much stuff he's packing away!"

Jessica glanced in the window at the booth just on the opposite side of the glass, saw the occupants, and her hand flew to her mouth. "Oohhh!"

"Why, Jessica, what's the matter?" Diana asked.

* * *

Hope stared at the reflection in the window of the drugstore — it was of herself and Peter. They stood side by side, hands locked together. Seen from the back, she supposed they'd give the impression of a happy couple, secure in their relationship with each other. But from the front, something was missing. Their facial expressions were like those of the mannequins in the window of the clothes store next door. Why? We are out *together* and we should be happy. Instead we look like we're — bored?

Glancing sideways at Peter, Hope wondered if he noticed their lifeless reflection. And if he did, whether it bothered him.

Peter was looking at a reflection all right, but it was of a Tarenton High junior. Standing across the mall with a couple of her friends, she was like a magnet, drawing everyone's attention. She seemed vivacious and carefree. Her long blonde hair swung behind her appealingly as she talked with great animation. Everything she said to her friends seemed to send them into peals of laughter. What was it about some girls that made them stand out like that and draw the attention of every guy for 50 feet around? Including me, he thought, feeling traitorous.

With a quick glance at Hope, to see if she was done with her apparent scrutiny of the items displayed in the drugstore window, he was surprised to see she was looking straight at him. Had she noticed where his attention had been aimed?

In hopes of distracting her if she had, he tugged gently on her hand and suggested, "Hey, I could sure use some liquid refreshment. How about we go grab a Coke or something?"

"Sure," Hope said, because she knew he wanted her to. But in reality she wanted more than anything just to ask him to take her home. If she did that, though, he'd ask if anything was wrong, and she wasn't sure if she was ready to confide in him all the disquieting thoughts that had been plaguing her lately. It actually took less energy to go with him.

They approached the first place that offered food and drink, the Farm Shop, and as the people who'd been walking in front of them turned off to the side to enter a store, another pair of shoppers was revealed standing directly in Hope and Peter's path. From the back, one of them was unmistakably Jessica Bennett. Then, suddenly, with no warning, Jessica spun on her heel and collided with Hope, knocking her to the ground.

"Oh! I'm sorry! I didn't see you," Jessica apologized in a choked voice.

"Be careful, Jessica. You need to watch where you're going," Peter reproved her. He bent to help Hope to her feet. "Are you okay?"

"Yeah," Hope replied, feeling slightly dazed. She was fine, but in a flash she realized this was the perfect opportunity to get Peter to take her home. "That is, I'll be fine if I can go home and lie down," she said, trying to look like a person in need of rest.

"Oh, Hope, did I hurt you?" Jessica looked horrified.

Hope felt like a heel for not being more honest. But this was her ticket out of here and she wasn't going to turn it down. "No, I'm just a little . . . uh . . . breathless. Just need to lie down and I'll be fine. Really, don't worry about me *at all*." She turned, hanging onto Peter's arm and allowed him to lead her away toward an exit.

Peter cast a disapproving look at Jessica, then turned all his attention to Hope.

Jessica stared after the couple leaving, feeling ten times worse than she had felt seeing Mary Ellen sitting with Patrick.

Then, to her further chagrin, the girl beside her asked, "Goodness, Jessica. What was all that about? I thought we were going to go in for a drink."

"Um, I have to get home. I just remembered. My mother needs something right away. Forgot what time it was," Jessica mumbled disjointedly at Diana and, turning yet a second time, said over her shoulder, "See you in school," and beat a hasty retreat right out of the mall.

There was one thing she was not going to allow happen, and that was finding herself sitting with Patrick and Mary Ellen. They may not still be in love, as he'd tried to tell her often enough, but that look on Mary Ellen's face, so intense, so filled with raw emotion, was enough to convey to Jessica that they still shared some kind of feelings — whatever they might be. And Jessica just didn't want to barge in on them when they seemed to be having such an intimate conversation. If

Patrick was an honest guy, he'd tell her later about the meeting.

And if he didn't mention it? Well. . . . Jessica shook herself and told herself staunchly that he *would* tell her. He'd told her to trust him, and that was what she was going to do.

CHAPTER

Tara felt immune to the noise in the halls of Tarenton High School. I'm like an island of quiet, she thought dreamily. But she wasn't alone on her island — there was a handsome blond man with wonderful blue eyes right beside her, and he thought she was the most fascinating creature he'd ever stumbled across. Or, more accurately, *run* into, Tara thought, giggling. Then she had to stifle the giggle. Giggling to yourself in the halls when you were all alone made kids think you were spaced out or something.

Nick Stewart. His name played like a much-loved song in Tara's brain. In fact, it blotted out everything else, including the voice of a classmate who was trying to get her attention.

"Tara Armstrong!" the voice said loudly as a hand waved in front of Tara's face.

"Huh?" She stopped short to prevent herself from plowing right into Holly Hudson. Holly, the

47

head of the Pompon Squad, sometimes helped the cheerleaders invent cheers; in fact, she had quite a talent for it. So naturally Tara thought the first words out of Holly's mouth would be about cheerleading.

"Isn't he a hunk?" Holly said, hugging her books to her chest as if she wished they were really the "hunk" in question.

Tara stared at her dumbly. "Who? Who?"

"What's with the owl impression?" Holly giggled, and then realized Tara honestly didn't know what she was talking about. "I asked, Isn't the new teacher a hunk?" At Tara's continued bemused expression she asked, "You mean you haven't heard? I thought the news about him would be around school by five minutes before first period, at the latest."

Tara was getting impatient. She didn't like not knowing what the conversation was about, and especially she didn't like not being up on the latest gossip, whether it was about a new teacher or whatever. That she, Tara Armstrong, didn't have the dope on some tidbit of news was impossible. Holly probably didn't know what she was talking about.

"There isn't a new teacher in our class," Tara objected firmly, and shoved a lock of red hair out of her eyes. She prepared to sidestep Holly in an attempt to get to her second-period class before the late bell rang.

To Tara's further aggravation, Holly just laughed. "I can't believe it," she said, shaking her head. "Of course there isn't a new teacher in *our* class. He's a math teacher for ninth grade. Remember Mrs. Adamson? Well, she had her baby last Friday night, a month early. So over the weekend they had to come up with a substitute *fast*. And I, for one, can't think of a better choice. I saw him just now down the hall, and I assumed you had, too, from that dreamy look in your eyes. Did you see him? Because if you did, forget trying to get him. The line has already formed and I'm number one hundred and five." She started giggling again, making her dark hair swing from side to side.

"No, I didn't see the teacher," Tara said shortly. "I suppose I'll see him eventually. But I really don't care how many girls are in the line because no matter how cute he is, I won't be joining it. I'm not into ancient relics. I like my men wrinkle-free." She laughed at her own joke and again tried to get by Holly.

"Oh, then you're in luck," Holly insisted. "This guy's so young I'll bet he still has to ask his mother's permission to go out." She sighed and looked in the direction where this paragon of looks and youth was supposed to have been minutes before.

Just then the bell rang and they had to dash for their next class.

"Well, I'm still not interested, so you can all have him," Tara called and ran for her English class. Her mind was just too full of a certain guy who had trouble steering a shopping cart. Smiling to herself, she pushed in the door and scooted into her seat before the teacher could turn from the blackboard and catch her.

The cheerleaders were doing their warm-up exercises when Coach Engborg came in, lugging her portable tape deck and a box of tissues. Her nose was red and her eyes, watery.

"Okay, kids, led's go," she said in a thickened voice.

"Gosh, Coach Engborg, you look truly pathetic," Tara commented upon catching sight of their coach. Ardith Engborg usually looked energetic, her small, compact body giving the impression it was capable of perpetual motion, but right now she looked as if she were ready to retire and move south.

"Thanks, Tara, for the kind words. Led me do the same for you sometime," her coach answered without rancor. She placed the tape player down and began playing a cassette of some of their favorite musical pieces. "Since, as one of you has so kindly pointed out, I look 'truly pathetic,' and since thad just happens to match the way I feel — " she took time out to blow her nose lustily " — I think we'll have a shortened practice session. I feel so tired I can't stand up for more than a few minutes ad a time. And since we don't have a game until next week, I thought you could use the break."

The kids looked at her as if her cold had affected her brain. Was this the same slave driver

50

who wouldn't be happy unless they achieved perfection?

Her cold must really be bad, Jessica thought, to let us leave early. Her heart skipped a beat as momentarily she thought that this would give her a few extra minutes to go over the books with Patrick for his moving business. Until she remembered that she hadn't talked to him since she'd spotted him with Mary Ellen in the mall yesterday. He hadn't called her last night, which he did often when they hadn't seen each other for a whole day. Her green eyes grew troubled. If he hadn't called her, then it was because he'd been busy. With what — or was it more accurate to say, with *whom*? Sighing deeply, she forced her mind to concentrate on what Coach Engborg was telling the kids.

A bunch of Tarenton students had come in to watch the squad practice. It was something that Coach considered desirable, since she felt it simulated what it was like to perform before a crowd at games, to some extent. One of the onlookers was Diana Tucker. Tara glared in her direction, disliking the way she always seemed to haunt the squad. And Diana's predatory expression was not one Tara liked seeing. What was she up to, anyway?

"All right, kids, led's go; led's do the 'Spirit' cheer." Their coach's voice, muffled by a Kleenex, sent the cheerleaders into action.

Sean, standing next to Tara, gazed up into the stands and also spotted Diana. Despite his

51

attempts to make a date with her when she'd first moved into town, she had shown no interest in starting up anything with him. It wasn't that he thought she was someone he particularly wanted to get to know, especially after the dirty tricks she'd played on some members of the squad, like Tara. What bothered him, what frustrated him, was to have a failure on his record. He felt sure his dad, the top salesman for Tarenton Fabricators, Tarenton's major business, didn't have any failures on *his* record. If he did, he certainly never told his son about them. All Sean ever heard about were the successes, the conquests.

Sean gave Diana one last look before concentrating on the old standby cheer.

"Got spirit?
Let's hear it!"

The squad went into a rousing, energetic cheer, designed to get the blood of both players and audience pumping.

Watching the six do the intricate flips and pyramids they did so well, Diana mused to herself. Yes, if Jessica were preoccupied enough, Diana thought, then her timing would be off. That maneuver that had her ending a flip by jumping up on Sean's legs for a flashy arch just might end in a miscalculation. Certainly it would be a disastrous miscalculation, and the worst that could happen would be — what? A broken leg? Yes, Diana decided, envisioning Jessica put out of commission by a nice big leg cast. *That* would certainly be a way of getting Jessica off the squad. So . . . Diana was just going to have to add fuel to the fire she'd started yesterday.

She waited until the kids took a break for a drink of water and a well-deserved rest, and then ambled toward the door, which also just happened to be in the same direction Jessica's feet were taking her. Jessica had a preoccupied air about her, and her normally sparkling green eyes seemed shadowed. Shrewdly observing Jessica's expression, Diana decided that the time was indeed ripe.

"Hello, there," she said, sounding chummy. "Did you make it home on time yesterday?"

Jessica looked at the attractive blonde as if she hadn't been aware that Diana was even in the gym.

"What? Oh, yes. I did." She prepared to keep moving, heading for a drinking fountain. Today she had no desire to engage in any kind of conversation with anyone.

But Diana had other desires.

"It's a shame we never got that drink together, Jessica. The shakes at the Farm Shop were as good as I had been told. Patrick seemed to feel — "

Jessica's head whipped around at the sound of his name.

"You went there after I left?" she asked, trying to sound only marginally interested.

"Oh, well, I was thirsty," Diana prevaricated. She'd done nothing of the sort. "He really can eat, can't he?" she observed with a laugh. Carelessly tossing her long blonde hair behind her, she added, "Mary Ellen seemed to think he was practically guilty of gluttony." The introduction of that name achieved the desired effect. Jessica looked as if she'd just been slapped. Diana rushed on, weaving her web of false impressions, before Jessica had a chance to speak. "Don't you admire a girl like Mary Ellen? Of course I never really got a chance to meet her until yesterday. I hadn't realized what a knockout she is. And she has so much city sophistication. I'll bet there isn't a guy in this dinky old town who sees her and doesn't instantly fall in love. Don't you agree?" She stared at Jessica, smiling as if they were simply engaged in idle school gossip rather than a subject designed to break Jessica's heart.

And Jessica did feel pain. Since Diana's observations so closely paralleled her own about Mary Ellen, she felt even worse. Could there be a guy in all of Tarenton who, if he wasn't already mad about Mary Ellen, could resist her allure? Even if he already had a girl friend?

Mumbling an indistinct reply, Jessica pushed through the doors and stumbled down the hall toward the drinking fountain. She had to stop doing this to herself. Hadn't Patrick told her time and again that his feelings for Mary Ellen were a thing of the past? So why couldn't she believe him? Why, every single time Mary Ellen came back to town, did Jessica fall off the cliff into the valley of her fears all over again?

Diana made no attempt to follow Jessica. She'd

done enough for today; any more might be over-kill. And this had to be accomplished at just the right speed to do the right amount of damage.

Smiling to herself in satisfaction, she turned and walked out through the front doors and into the sunlight. Several male heads turned to watch in admiration as she passed. Diana knew she was attractive to them, but she wanted *more* than male approval. She wanted to be in the limelight. It was tough being the new girl in town and having to scrape and claw to get kids to accept her. Diana had learned early in her school career that the only way to get accepted by the student body in any school was to be someone so special everybody wanted to know you. Popularity — spelled out all in *capitals*! That's what she wanted. And, if everything went as she planned, very soon now she just might be well on her way — as a cheer-leader.

CHAPTER

After practice, Sean proposed that the squad take advantage of the extra time off Coach Engborg had given them by going out for Cokes or something.

"Face it, none of our folks expect us home until after six, anyway," he said with a careless shrug.

Jessica, Olivia, and Tara decided it was a good idea.

Hope, however, asked Peter in a low voice if he'd take her home. She really needed the extra time for homework, she told him.

Watching Peter and Hope walk to Peter's car, Jessica thought how solid a couple they were. She felt a stab of jealousy as she thought of Patrick. There had been a time when she thought she and Patrick were as solid as Peter and Hope. But now she wasn't sure.

* * *

Solid was not exactly the word Hope would have used to describe her relationship with Peter lately. At her house, where he opened the door for her, she avoided looking into his eyes. Could he read her face? she wondered. Walking slowly into the house, she thought, Something is very wrong. Here I am, actually happy that I came home immediately after practice instead of going somewhere with Peter. But there *was* that paper to write for English literature. And she did need to practice her violin. Stifling a sigh, she waited at the door and forced herself to look at Peter this time.

Funny, Peter thought. Hope looks just as cute as she always has, yet I am not really sorry that she didn't want to hang out somewhere after Mrs. Engborg let us out early. I'm actually relieved that now I have more time to work on that social studies assignment. I must be certifiable if I'd prefer hacking out a piece of useless garbage for some ridiculous teacher than spending time with Hope.

"Well, I . . . uh . . . guess I'll see you tomorrow," he said slowly.

Hope looked at him, feeling like a hypocrite. She almost wanted to ask Peter to come inside and talk it out. She wanted to tell him, Look, Peter, I don't know for sure if you and I are right for each other anymore. I'm beginning to feel something's not quite the same. I'm even wondering if perhaps there are two people out there who could make better matches for us than we've always thought we were. But for all she knew, he didn't feel the same way, and if she told him how she felt, he'd be hurt. It could all be in her mind. And if it was, then she was the one who had to sort things out.

"Yeah," she murmured.

Peter lowered his mouth to kiss her good-bye.

Hope raised her head to receive the kiss, thinking, I used to like Peter's kisses so much. They were still nice, but. . . . She refused to carry the thought further. Once she was inside, away from Peter, maybe she could analyze the problem more clearly.

They parted, each turning away without further conversation.

Driving away from the Chang residence, Peter thought to himself, What's wrong with our romance lately? It seems to have lost its spark. We have as much excitement between us as there is between a couple of fish. Why? What was wrong? Was it his fault? Or Hope's? Or were both of them to blame?

Lying against the bolster of her day bed, Hope stared idly into space. She'd made no effort to bring out her violin or to start on that writing assignment. Instead she was mulling over the problem with Peter. Did she still like him? Yes, she decided firmly. Peter was very likable. But love? She wasn't sure anymore. There was a time when if she didn't see Peter first thing in the morning as soon as she got to school, the rest of the day seemed to lack something vital. Just the *thought* of Peter used to make her feel happiness coursing through her veins. And the very fact that she now had doubts about the strength of her feelings for him, the boy she'd been dating for months, upset her greatly.

To whom could she talk about this? Her fellow cheerleaders? Some of them had certainly experienced romantic breakups. Olivia had actually been dumped by that guy Walt from last year's Varsity Squad. Then there was Sean, who'd had problems with at least three girls this year. And Jessica? No, she was just starting out on her romance with Patrick. And besides, she'd never been serious about any boy before him. What about Tara? No, she'd never *really* had a strong relationship with a guy she cared about, either.

Actually, Hope didn't really want to have a heart-to-heart talk with anyone on the squad — not when her problem was with *one* of the squad. So who did that leave? Her parents? Definitely not, she decided. They'd gotten over their initial resistance to her dating Peter, even though he wasn't Asian, as they were. But she wasn't sure that if she were to confide in them that her relationship with Peter wasn't as solid as it used to be, her parents wouldn't take the opportunity to try to convince her to look for a new boyfriend from among the few Asians they knew.

Hope flopped over and stared out the window in defeat. This was just something that she was going to have to try to forget and hope it sorted itself out. She didn't know what else to do.

The rest of the squad had opted to go to the

Pizza Palace. Since there were only four of them, they took a booth and sat around talking about their cheerleading routines and making bets on how long their coach would allow her cold to get the best of her.

"Guaranteed, by tomorrow's practice, she'll be on so many antibiotics she'll be her old slave-driver self again," Sean commented, a wry grin on his lifeguard-handsome face.

"Yeah, and we'll be our old exhausted selves again," Tara agreed, smiling back.

They all knew the major reason they were considered such a dynamite squad was because Coach Engborg never settled for less than what she considered to be their best.

After they'd been there about a half hour, Olivia looked at her watch and said, "Ugh! Guess it's time to be heading home."

"Yeah," Jessica said reluctantly. For her to go home meant one of two things: Either she'd find out that Patrick called (and she wasn't sure how she'd respond to that); or she could look forward to yet another great conversation with her stepfather that would run like this: "Jessica, I saw a new pair of shoes on your feet this morning. Where did the money for them come from?" And she'd answer, "Well, uh, Mom had a little extra in her paycheck this week because she worked overtime one day and she — " At which point her stepfather would say to Abby, his wife, "So why didn't that get put toward some bills?" By then Jessica would be exerting herself to keep from snapping at him saying, "We didn't fall into debt before you came along, and we're not about to do it now." That would definitely not endear her to Daniel, and it would certainly hurt her mother. Sighing, she flexed her toes in her new cobalt blue flats, and rose, gathering her belongings.

"Yeah, I gotta breeze, too," Sean said. His dad was actually going to be home for dinner tonight, and Windy, their nickname for Mrs. Windsor, their housekeeper, had promised to produce something really outstanding for their meal. Sharing a meal with his father was such a rare occasion, Sean had no intention of missing it.

Tara rose to follow Olivia, who was leading the group from the place, and then halfway to the door realized she'd left her coat in the booth.

"Hey, guys, I just forgot something. Wait for me outside. I'll be right there."

Since she was giving Jessica and Olivia a ride, they said, "Okay," and turned to head out the door.

Sean called, "See you later," and left.

Tara's coat was squashed up against the corner right where she'd been sitting. Picking it up, she turned to leave Kenny's once again — and almost collided with Nick Stewart a second time!

"Oh!" she said. "Hi!" She was immediately disgusted at the amount of enthusiasm she'd allowed to show in her voice. Tara believed in acting cool toward boys.

But Nick seemed equally happy to see her.

Reaching out to keep her from being knocked over, he braced her with his hands on her upper arms. Tara liked the feeling.

"Well, hello there, gourmet lady," he said, smiling widely. "Uh, did your housekeeper accomplish her appointed task successfully the other night?"

"Huh? Oh, yes, of course. Marie always does everything to perfection," Tara said with a dismissive wave of her hand. Simply parroting what her parents often said, she was unaware of how grown-up she sounded. But Marie and her work were not exactly among the top ten subjects Tara wanted to talk about at the moment. What she wanted to talk about was this gorgeous man. She was positive, on second meeting, that he attended college, perhaps the nearby junior college, since he'd told her he'd just moved into town recently — in fact, the past weekend. Maybe he was a transfer student, although why anyone would transfer to Hillsborough when they could go to college in some major city, she couldn't fathom. She wanted to know all about him; he'd been on her mind almost exclusively since they met, so why not have a few details?

"I was just checking out your recommendation of this place as a great pizza place," he informed her. His wide grin showed wonderfully straight teeth.

"Oh, great," Tara answered, then added with a sly smile, "but, uh, if you get ptomaine poisoning, please don't sue me," she joked.

"What? You mean you lied?" Nick pretended to look aghast.

"No, no, it's just . . . well . . . you never know if someone is going to like a place as well as you do. This place does have the best-tasting pizza in town, but there are places that are cheaper and — " she looked around and added under her breath " — less full of the . . . um . . . school crowd." If she made it sound like she herself was not a member of that "school crowd," maybe he'd be more inclined to be interested in her. She *hoped*!

"Y–e–a–h," Nick said slowly, with a glance around at the occupants of the place. Although it was early, there were still quite a lot of students from Tarenton High there, and it looked like their presence was causing Nick to feel uncomfortable.

Tara wanted to tell him about some other place where there would be great pizza and fewer kids, but there weren't any. All the places that had good pizza just naturally drew kids. With a mental shrug, she decided not to say anything.

Then she remembered that Olivia and Jessica were outside waiting for her, and it was getting late. She wasn't free to hang around talking to Nick. Her parents weren't strict about her getting home for dinner, but they did expect her to be there unless there was a special reason for not doing so. And since her father was actually going to be home tonight instead of working late, she knew it was especially important that she be on time.

Besides, if she didn't get out in the parking lot quick, the other two girls would come looking for her, and the last thing she wanted was for either of them to spot Nick. After all, she'd seen him first.

"Oh, it's late and I have to go." Tara moaned as she glanced at her watch. She gazed at him apologetically and explained, "I really must get home. I sure hope you enjoy the pizza. Maybe the next time we run into each other you can tell me how you liked it here."

Nick laughed shortly, glanced at his own watch — which, Tara noticed absently, was on his right wrist — and quipped, "Okay, I'll see you later, Cinderella."

"What?" Tara asked, confused.

"You're always looking at your watch and running away. I'd love to see you sometime when it's broken."

Tara laughed and said, "Let me know when. I'll step on it." She hurried out of the Pizza Palace. He was so cute! She just had to see him again. But when would it be? And would they ever be more than simply two people who kept bumping into each other?

CHAPTER

8

When Jessica arrived home, she attempted to get upstairs and remove her shoes before Daniel saw them. Halfway up the stairs, she was beginning to congratulate herself on her success, when her plan fell through.

"Oh, hello, Jessica," Daniel greeted her, coming down the stairs.

"Oh! Um, hi," she said, attempting to get by her stepfather without him seeing the shoes — a neat trick that proved impossible.

Frowning slightly, Daniel's all-seeing eyes lit on the cobalt blue flats, and he stated, "New shoes." Oddly is was not a question, but rather a kind of resigned observation.

Here it comes! she thought dispiritedly. "Um, yeah." Then she added somewhat defiantly, "Mom bought them with the extra money she got in her paycheck last week for her overtime. They were part of a preseason sale — really a *bargain*," she emphasized.

Daniel gave them the once-over, then said in a tone of voice that she hadn't ever heard him use, "Yes, well, they're . . . unusual." And with that, he turned and proceeded on down the stairs!

Looking after him, Jessica's green eyes widened in astonishment. Who was *that* man? A clone someone had put in place of the real Daniel Bennett? Shaking her head slightly, she turned and continued on to her room. Maybe he wasn't feeling well and didn't have the strength to take her to the mat for allowing her mother to misspend her precious and hard-earned dollars, she thought with a bemused smile. She was certainly going to have to ask her mother about him later.

Olivia stood looking at the note her mother had left for her by the phone in her bedroom. One small hand was clenched at her side, while the other tortured a strand of her thick brown hair. The note was about David, and it was not a welcome message: "He's sorry he can't see you the rest of the week but something's come up and he won't be free until Sunday. Will call later to explain." Resisting the urge to tear the little scrap of paper into even smaller scraps and scatter them out the window in the wind, Olivia turned and walked out of her room and down the hall. Count to ten; recite the preamble to the Constitution; use transcendental meditation — but *don't*, whatever you do, think about why he can't fit you into his heavy schedule this week! she counseled herself.

Despite the fact that in about ten minutes they were going to sit down to dinner, Olivia took a cookie from the jar and ate it with gnashing, tearing bites. In her mind's eye the cookie was Jennifer Clark, and she wished she could mash her out of David's life as easily as she could destroy that cookie. There was no doubt in her mind what he was up to.

Well, she thought with a determined glint in her dark eyes, if David didn't have time for her, then she was just going to have to find someone who did. Starting tomorrow!

"O–o–o–h! There he is!" someone at the next lunch table moaned.

The cheerleaders, all gathered at their customary table, turned as a group to see what was sending the juniors at the table next to them into raptures.

"Oh, wow! Pinch me! Am I dreaming? Is he really that cute?"

"I wish I was back in ninth grade again. I never thought I'd say those words, but *he'd* make it all worthwhile," another girl sighed.

Tara turned to Hope, who was sitting next to her, and asked, "Hope, who are all those girls over there talking about?" She smiled slightly, thinking how silly juniors seemed to her now that she was a senior — with the exception of Hope, of course.

Hope sat up straighter and looked in the same direction as her classmates, then shrugged slightly and grinned. "Ah, yes. I should have guessed. Haven't you heard about that gorgeous new math teacher for ninth grade?"

"Oh, yeah," Tara said vaguely, remembering Holly's news the day before.

"Well, Mr. Perfect just joined the lunch line." She pointed for Tara's benefit, who now sat up straighter herself to get a look. "See? Over there by Mr. Delaney, the tenth grade math teacher?"

Tara looked to see "Mr. Perfect" and promptly choked on the bite of macaroni and cheese in her mouth. She started coughing and turning red, and everyone at the table became alarmed.

Pounding Tara on the back, Sean asked, "What happened? Go down the wrong pipe?"

"Are you okay?" Olivia asked.

Tara got herself under control, and then turned red for a different reason. Mr. Perfect was *her* Mr. Perfect — Nick Stewart! She'd die if he ever saw her here in the lunchroom! In fact, there was only one thing left for her to do — escape as fast as possible! Jumping to her feet, she exclaimed in a breathy voice, "Uh, I better go to the ladies' room. Think I need some air." She paused and looked a little wildly at Hope. "Would you return my tray?"

"Sure," Hope said, regarding Tara with a worried expression on her face.

"Is there anything I can do?" Jessica asked. "Do you need help?"

Oh, do I ever need help! Help being invisible!

Tara thought hysterically. "No, um, no." She turned, charting her course out of the lunchroom to take her as far from Nick's path as possible.

Once she was in the girls' room, Tara stared at the distraught reflection of herself in the mirror, and thought, How am I ever going to avoid being seen by Nick for the rest of the day — no, make that for the rest of my life! Her shoulders sagged. She didn't see how it was going to be possible. Oh, *why* did her "college guy" and the new knockout teacher have to be one and the same?

She stayed in the girls' room until the warning bell rang and then, feeling like someone on the ten most wanted list, she rushed to her next class. Somehow she was going to have to make it through the day without passing anywhere near the ninth grade math room. Even if she had to go down the wrong halls and take different staircases, there was no way on this earth she'd ever let Nick find out she was a *student!*

By the end of the day Tara's nerves felt French-fried. During cheerleading practice, she kept glancing toward the open doors leading to the hall, fearful that at any moment Nick would walk by and look in. Would he recognize her if she hung her head upside down and turned away? Probably not. But the trick would be spotting him before he —

"Tara!" Ardith Engborg said sharply.

"Huh?" Tara turned to her coach, eyes like saucers.

Coach Engborg was about to reprimand Tara

for her lack of concentration when she noticed the haunted expression on the girl's face. What was the matter with her? Rephrasing what she'd been about to say, Ardith Engborg commented as mildly as possible, "Could you please try to think about your moves?"

I am, Mrs. Engborg, but not the kind you have in mind, Tara thought darkly. She really tried to pay attention to her coach's instructions, but it proved a formidable task.

They were attempting to slightly revise one of their old cheers, and it took more concentration than usual since Coach Engborg wanted them to include some Arabian jumps in it. Jessica and Olivia had learned the Arabians in January, but now the rest of the squad was supposed to master the tricky maneuver. It required that they do a forward flip with a half twist before landing on their feet, and bad timing could make them fall on a shoulder — or worse, on their heads!

Ardith Engborg knew she was asking a lot to expect the whole squad to do them, but she felt they'd been working together and performing for a long enough time that they should be proficient enough to do it.

Sean and Peter were extremely pleased to be given the chance to do the fancy jumps. With Olivia giving them helping hints, they practiced on the mats until they felt dizzy. Hope wasn't as positive of her abilities as the guys were, but she tried gamely, despite her fears of crashing head-first any moment into a mat.

Jessica, however, was having as difficult a time

70

giving practice her full concentration as Tara was. Patrick had called the night before to tell her he wouldn't be able to finish his moving job in time to come by and pick her up today after practice. But that wasn't what was bothering her. It was the fact that not once during their conversation had he mentioned his being with Mary Ellen on Sunday. Not once! Did he feel he had something to hide? She'd listened carefully to his tone of voice to see if it sounded different than usual, but it was really impossible to tell over the phone. When he'd suggested they go to the movies this weekend, she'd almost felt like saying no. After all, did she want to date a guy who kept secrets? But then she'd reasoned, if she went with him, maybe *then* he'd say something about Mary Ellen.

This is stupid! she berated herself as she faltered coming out of the Arabian jump and landed slightly off balance. I have got to stop brooding about that girl and think about what I'm doing right now. Otherwise I'm going to get hurt. Especially if I fall doing one of these Arabians.

Diana Tucker, peering in from the hallway, was thinking exactly the same thing.

CHAPTER

The cheerleaders were exhausted when six o'clock finally arrived and Mrs. Engborg allowed them to stop.

"Not bad, kids," she said gruffly, well aware of the drain learning those Arabians had been for some of them. "By the end of practice tomorrow you should be able to perform them fairly well. We'll have a run-through, and if you're good enough I may decide you can use them at our next game, on Monday. Now beat it and get some rest," she ended, giving them a smile before turning to walk to her office.

Various moans and groans accompanied the six cheerleaders exiting the gymnasium.

"Hey, you were really great," someone said close to Olivia's head as she came out through the gym doors.

Startled, she turned to find Red Butler standing there smiling at her. Red got his nickname because his hair rivaled Tara's for color. But the kids also got a charge out of calling him "Red" Butler because it was so close to the name of Rhett Butler, the hero of *Gone with the Wind*.

Red wasn't exactly thrilled about the name, but he accepted it with good humor. In fact, he was a guy with a sense of humor almost as zany as David's, and Olivia liked him.

"Thanks," Olivia said with a tired smile. She wondered why he'd stayed after to talk to her. Then she remembered the resolve she'd made the night before after reading the phone message concerning David — the very phone message that said he'd call "later," which he hadn't. She looked at Red a little more closely.

"You watch practice often?" she asked, aiming a radiant smile straight at him.

He returned the smile, and since she seemed to be in a friendly mood, he started walking toward the stairwell with her. "Yeah, and all the games. You guys make even a bad game interesting."

"Oh, wow! What praise!" Olivia said with a laugh. Cocking her head to give him a sideways look, she added, "Stick around. I could use the good words. Coach Engborg can be a little heavy on the criticism and a little lean on the compliments sometimes." The femme fatale at work, she thought drolly. It was a role she wasn't exactly used to playing. Maybe this was the time to learn. She'd seen Tara in fine form often enough to have picked up a few pointers.

Taking her conversation as a sign of interest,

Red walked her all the way to the girls' locker room door.

"I'd be glad to. Watching you in action is worth it!" he said as they descended the stairs.

"That's it," Olivia exclaimed. "How much do you charge an hour to dole out compliments like that?"

Red laughed and said, "Oh, I come real cheap."

They paused at the locker room door, reluctant to have this promising conversation end. Red had always admired Olivia, and had wished on several occasions that she'd see him as more than the class clown.

Olivia looked up at him, thinking he wasn't really bad-looking. In fact, that red hair was his only drawback in her opinion. She had been partial to blonds lately. But then she wasn't having much luck with the one blond in her life, so maybe she ought to change her preferences.

Smiling encouragingly at him, she asked, "Say, you drive a car to school, don't you?"

"Yeah." He frowned, puzzled at this change of topic.

"Well, could I ask you for a lift home?"

"Sure you can."

"May I have a lift home?" she asked, laughing at his humorous expression.

"Hey, yeah, you sure can." His grin widened in surprise mixed with pleasure.

"I'll be out as soon as I can," she promised, and pushed in the door to the locker room, giving him a small wave.

"Take your time," he said generously, and then turned to walk back upstairs. Whistling to himself, he sat down to wait on the steps outside the front door of the school.

"That's wild," Hope was saying to Jessica, as Olivia came into the locker room.

"What's wild?" Olivia asked. She stepped back to avoid being dripped on by Tara, who was coming out of the shower trying to dry her masses of thick red hair. Sprays of water droplets were being flung off her head as she vigorously rubbed at her hair with a towel.

"Jessica was just telling me about her step-father. Seems he's gone through a personality change," Hope explained.

"Well, it was probably only temporary," Jessica said with a dry laugh. She told Olivia about his reaction to her new shoes the night before, then added, "So I asked my mom about it and she said she'd already told him about the shoes and how she paid for them. He'd started to argue with her, then suddenly said, 'Well, you earn the money, I guess you should have *some* say about how it's spent.' My mom about fainted from surprise. I mean, *Daniel*, actually starting to loosen up about money."

"It must be a miracle," Olivia said, laughing. "But seriously, I hope it lasts."

"I do, too," Jessica agreed heartily. It had been nice at the time, but she figured it probably wasn't permanent.

Tara peeked out of the locker room before

75

actually stepping into the hall, saw it was clear, and sprinted over to the stairs, practically racing up them. She slowed down at the top, once again checking for signs of Nick Stewart, saw none, and ran for the door. Outside, she saw that the grounds and parking lot were practically empty. Now, to make it to her car and away from the school, and she'd be home free!

Five minutes later she was driving down Main Street, breathing a sigh of relief. How she was going to make it through school the rest of the week was beyond her. Then, glancing at her gas gauge, she thought to herself a little dryly, How I'm going to make it home is a bigger problem. Once again she'd forgotten to check the gauge and right now it looked like the car was running on fumes. Spying the Mobil station on the next block, Tara hoped she'd make it that far.

Thankfully she did, and, expelling a breath she hadn't even been aware she'd been holding, she drove up next to a pump. Then she saw that an older model MG was already being filled from it. Even though the little sports car was not new, it was still really classy. Tara took a moment to admire it, then glanced at its owner.

Her breath lodged painfully in her throat. Oh, no! It just couldn't happen again!

Nick Stewart! Oh, help!

Then she got herself together. What was the matter with her? This wasn't school. In fact it was almost on the opposite side of town from school. She was safe here.

Before she could finish deciding if she should

say anything to him, he turned to replace the nozzle on the pump, spotted her, and exclaimed, "Well, we meet again!" Then, with a mischievous glance around, he joked, "But, uh, I don't think they sell gourmet gas here."

Tara laughed in delight. His wry comment showed that the place where he'd first met her was becoming a standard joke between them. "Well, I guess the poor car will just have to do with the same gas as the peasants put in theirs," she replied, pushing her silky red hair from her face.

They smiled at each other, knowing their conversation was silly.

"How was the pizza?" Tara thought to ask.

"Oh, well, I decided to forget it. It was kind of crowded there, with . . . ah . . . kids a little young for my tastes." He made this admission a little sheepishly, but Tara understood perfectly — now!

She nodded her head, and agreed, "Yeah, I know what you mean," hoping she sounded convincing.

Nick subjected her to a searching look, and then said slowly, "Say, I was thinking. I'm kind of getting tired of seeing you only when we run into each other. How about we do something on purpose for a change and go somewhere for a drink to get acquainted?" He shrugged and added, with an appealing look, "Since you know so much about this town, you could share some more of your knowledge with me. Sort of to help a new guy out. What do you say?" He'd come over to stand next to her as he'd talked, and now was within close enough range so she could see the shadow of his beard — as she should have expected from someone old enough to be a *teacher*. But along with that, she was close enough to see his stunningly attractive features only too well, and he was impossible to resist.

A drink. What kind of a drink did he have in mind? What kind of drink would most teachers have in mind after being in class all day? Coffee? Don't kid yourself, Tara thought ruefully. If coffee was what Nick had in mind, he would have said coffee. An alcoholic drink, maybe? It was after six o'clock, so she guessed it wasn't too early for a guy his age to want one. But if an alcoholic drink was what he had in mind, she couldn't go with him anywhere they sold them. She was underage. What should she do?

"So how about it?" he prompted, reaching to pick up the gas nozzle for her.

Whether it was the warm touch of his hand or the attractive look on his face, Tara didn't know, but before she could stop herself, she said, "Sure, why not?"

Why not indeed! Tara, you maniac! she told herself.

"Great! We'll hit the road as soon as I gas up this . . . um . . . beauty of a car," he said, teasing her gently about her older-model car, and obviously extremely pleased that she'd agreed.

All she did was stare at him, not trusting herself to speak without her voice shaking. I am certifiably mad, she thought, watching him fill the car, then replace the nozzle.

"I'll just go pay for this," she said hastily, and walked briskly into the gas station to hand the clerk the money.

Where would they go? she fretted. Would he expect her to suggest a place since she was the native? If he did, what would she say? What *could* she say? She knew all the places that served alcoholic beverages; that was common knowledge, but. . . .

Fortunately she didn't have to say anything, because as soon as she got back to Nick, he said, "Come on, follow me. Over the weekend I discovered this really neat place. Of course, you probably already know about it. It's called Class Act. Right now it'll be dead, which is just fine with me. We can talk easier that way." He grinned at her, and with difficulty she smiled back at him.

"Class Act? Um, sure, I know it." At least I know where it is, she amended herself. She knew it was a small place on the edge of town that served more than beverages; it also served sandwiches. But she'd never stepped foot in it her entire life!

Oh, well, she thought, there's a first time for everything. And she just didn't want to miss out on being with Nick as much as she could. Maybe, just maybe, she could get him to like her so much, that if — no, in all honesty she knew that was *when* — he found out she was a student, he wouldn't want to give her up, despite the fact that *he* was a *teacher* and *she* was a *student*.

CHAPTER

Mary Ellen Kirkwood came out of the hospital, looking haggard and drawn. Being by her mother's bedside for the better part of the day had taken its toll. But now that her mother was out of the woods, she was free to go and see about finding something to cook for her dad for dinner when he came home from his bus route.

As she was about to step off the curb, a horn blast made her stop in midstep.

Patrick, in his garbage truck, was grinning at her and waving from across the street. Smiling tiredly, she hurried over to the truck and got in. It was amazing how a little experience in life, like living with two other girls in a one-bedroom apartment in New York City, could mature her enough so sitting in a garbage truck didn't make her cringe as it had only last year.

"Hi, there," Patrick said. "Just come from seeing your mom?"

Mary Ellen nodded, sighing, "Yes. I've been there almost all day."

"How's she doing?"

"Fine, now. They were a little worried because she took so long to come out of the anaesthesia, but now she's awake and seems to be doing okay. She told me to go home and feed my dad." She smiled at Patrick, who put the truck in gear and drove away from the curb.

"Well, guess that's my next stop," he said, grinning. He knew Mary Ellen was over her revulsion to riding in his rig now, and was glad. Since they'd talked on Sunday and she'd told him the news about her mother, who was having gall-bladder surgery, he'd made it a point to be in a position to give her a lift to the hospital yesterday. He was glad that he'd run across her just now and could help her out again. Their relationship would probably never be as loose and easy as it would have been had they not had a short, tempestuous romance, but at least now they could talk like two normal human beings.

"So when do you go back to the big city?" he asked.

"Well, I guess I'll be going back in a couple of days, for a while. I've got some interviews and one small modeling job. Then it's unemployment time again," she added with a wry laugh. "I'll probably come back from time to time to see how Mom's doing and to help out around the house. Gemma can't do it all, and Dad can't take time off from his bus route. And after Mom gets home, she really shouldn't be doing anything for a couple of weeks."

"So, you'll be back in town, huh? Well, maybe I'll see you," Patrick said easily.

"Of course you will!" Mary Ellen said feelingly. She reached out to give Patrick a one-armed hug, wishing he'd get over this stiffness around her. As far as she was concerned, she felt their past was exactly that — their *past* — time to forget all that had gone on between them, time for the present, and the future. She smiled dreamily to herself, thinking about another meeting she wanted soon. But not with Patrick.

With a start, Jessica Bennett jumped back against the door to the stationery store. Her arms tightened convulsively around the bag she was holding, containing billing forms she'd just bought for Patrick to use in his two businesses, moving and garbage. A painful tightness formed in her throat as she watched the white garbage truck go by, round the corner at the end of the block, and disappear from view. But she couldn't get the image in her mind to disappear.

Mary Ellen. In Patrick's truck. With her arm around him! Where were they going? Jessica knew his route today and she knew this street wasn't on it.

She wanted to march over to the trash can placed at the edge of the street and dump the forms she'd just bought. He'd called her last night to ask her to pick them up and she'd agreed, trying valiantly to give him the benefit of the doubt. Maybe she'd been guilty of making a mountain out of a molehill again, she'd told herself. Maybe there was nothing to Mary Ellen and Patrick eating together in the Farm Shop on Sunday. She'd almost gotten herself to believe it. But then, to come out of the stationery store, after the little task Patrick had assigned her, and find him with Mary Ellen's arm around him!

"Ohhh!" She expelled the sound with an angry breath and strode down the street to where she'd parked her mother's car. Tossing the forms violently into the passenger side, she dropped into the driver's seat and tried calming down before starting the car. It would never do to get into an accident. She could get killed. Then she'd never get the chance to tell Patrick off!

Diana Tucker was at the light on Main and Maple when Patrick's garbage truck drove by. She smiled. Mary Ellen and Patrick, together in his garbage truck. How cozy. And what a gift it was for Diana to witness this event. Continuing to smile, Diana crossed the street and gave careful thought to the exact way she would phrase this revelation to Jessica tomorrow at school, and also to when would be the most effective time to reveal it. Right before Jessica went to perform some complicated routine was obviously the best possible time. But the wording had to be just right. . . .

Tara stared across the table at Nick Stewart's incredibly handsome face and thought to herself:

I'm here with a *teacher*! I must need my head examined.

"What can I get you folks?" a pretty waitress asked them.

Nick smiled up at her, and said, "I'll have whatever you have on tap. And the lady. . . ." He raised his adorable dark blond eyebrows at Tara questioningly.

"Um, I'll have . . . a Coke," she finally said. She hoped that Nick wouldn't wonder about her soft drink order in a place that patently catered to the bar crowd.

Nick looked at her, his eyes narrowed in perplexity. The waitress went off and Nick said, "A Coke? Don't tell me you're a teetotaler."

What was the right answer to that? she thought frantically. She had to make him think she was older than she was, but she didn't want to sound judgmental, either. Then she had it. "I have to drive, and since I really don't feel like buying a replacement for my present set of wheels, I think I'll just drive sober." She gazed at him with as much innocence as she could muster.

He laughed and sat back, relaxing against the back of the booth. "Ah," he said, as if that explained everything. "Very smart."

Tara breathed a tiny breath of relief, and forced herself to ask, "So, tell me, what brought you to Tarenton?" She knew very well, but she couldn't let on that she did, could she?

Nick launched into an explanation that took the better part of the next thirty minutes, complete with anecdotes about his interview with Mrs.

Oetjen, with Tara trying hard not to look like she knew personally the high school principal.

"So she asked me why I thought I'd be able to take over the math teacher's job when I hadn't had any teaching experience," Nick was saying, "and I told her I had five younger brothers and sisters and I had to tutor them in math, so I felt that qualified me."

They both laughed.

"Five! How did you survive? I'm an only child," Tara prompted. Keep the guy talking, that was the only way.

"You are, eh? Well . . ." and Nick went off on that tangent, telling Tara about some of the silly things his siblings did.

They laughed and talked for another thirty minutes and the more he talked, the more she liked him. He was so amusing and animated, and by virtue of the fact that he was older and had gone to college, he had a lot of experiences he could talk about. In fact, she was beginning to feel like she was falling down a huge chasm, and didn't know where the bottom was. It was frightening. What was she going to do? Why couldn't he have been a boring talker, instead of someone so interesting?

He talked about how he'd saved his smallest sister's cat from a dog once, and how she'd thanked him by making his bed for a week. Shaking her head over that, Tara thought what a neat, caring guy he was!

The waitress came back to ask if they wanted refills for the second time, and Tara sneaked a peek at her watch. It was past dinnertime, and she'd have a lot of explaining to do when she got home. Looking at Nick, who was waiting to see if she wanted another drink, she said, "Oh, I . . . uh . . . have to go. It's — "

"Don't tell me," he interjected. "It's late. I'm beginning to think you're not Cinderella; you're the March Hare."

Tara smiled. "You mean that rabbit that was always late in *Alice in Wonderland*? Please, I'm not that bad, am I?" she asked with a laugh.

"Yes, you are that bad. But look, if you *have* to go, at least give me your phone number. I'm going to make it my business to snag you some-time when you don't have to run away."

"My phone number . . ." Tara said faintly. She swallowed and tried to come up with some reasonable-sounding excuse for not giving it to him, and failed. "All right," she said, writing it down for him on a scrap of paper from her purse. Handing it to him, she stood up to go.

He rose with her and walked her out of the place. At her car, he looked deeply into her eyes as if he was trying to read in them all about the real Tara Armstrong. She attempted to shield her eyes. Don't let him see how scared you are, or what a phony you are!

"I *will* see you again," he promised, smiling.

Tara turned and dropped into her gold Chevy, and smiled up at him from the driver's seat. "Sure," she said. But only she knew that it would be at *school*, with her luck!

He waved good-bye to her until she had driven around the corner and was out of sight.

All the way home she berated herself for getting into this mess. But it wasn't really all her fault, was it? After all, when he'd run into her at the grocery store she hadn't known then that he was a teacher. He was extremely young-looking. With a smile she remembered his tale about his first day at Tarenton, last Monday, when he'd been walking down the hall toward the lunchroom and one of the older teachers had come up to him and demanded to see his pass. His pass! They'd both enjoyed the joke.

But, oh, even though he *looked* young, he wasn't young. He was a teacher. It was one thing to have a crush on a teacher from a distance, but it was another thing to actually enter into a romance with one. There was no other way to describe that but as downright *insane*.

CHAPTER

"Red, Red, whatever shall I do? Shall I have a Coke or a Pepsi?" Olivia looked across the table at Red Butler, pretending to be a Southern belle unable to make a decision.

Red leaned across the table, trying to look solemn, and growled, "Frankly, my dear, Olivia, I don't give a darn." Then he grinned and added, "But make a choice fast; here comes our waitress." Actually, Red hated takeoffs on *Gone with the Wind*, but since Olivia didn't know that — he assumed — he played along with her.

"What'll you have, kids?" The waitress pushed a pencil into her hair, and stood on one leg as if her feet hurt. She regarded them with a tired look, which prompted Olivia to respond immediately, "A Coke, please." She tried not to laugh out loud until the woman went away.

Olivia and Red were at Burger Benny's, a popular hangout with the school crowd, and that crowd was considerable. When Red had driven Olivia home earlier, he'd asked her if she wanted to go out after dinner. All she'd needed to make her say yes was to remember how David hadn't been exactly sitting around pining for her lately. Why should she be hanging around all night waiting for a call from *him*? Especially since there wasn't a guarantee he'd do it. Besides, it was nice being with a guy who seemed to admire her so much. And if David did call and learned that she was out with Red, maybe it would make him think.

They sat there, talking for a while about school, and the one course they both took, although not the same period — chemistry, which they both hated.

"I always seem to turn out beakers full of stuff the wrong color," Olivia confided with a laugh. "Mr. Spencer must think I have the potential to be dangerous, because midsemester he gave me Steve Cohen as a lab partner."

"Oh, Steve," Red drawled with understanding.

"Steve's probably going to be an astrophysicist or something," Olivia joked. "His grade never falls below ninety-five in that class, and every time I'm about to do anything exciting, like blow up the lab, Steve's there to stop me."

They laughed, and then Olivia's laughter died in her throat as she watched two new people enter Benny's. She stared in shock as David and Jennifer sauntered through the room, David's blue eyes sweeping the place, until he spotted Olivia. Then he smiled widely, making his right cheek dimple. He actually looked happy to have found her, Olivia thought in surprise. If he were trying to avoid me, he wouldn't look that pleased, would he? As he came nearer, with a sulky-looking Jennifer close on his heels, she wondered what he'd think about finding her here with Red.

"Well, here you are," he said when they'd finally arrived at the booth. His blue gaze narrowed slightly on Red, sitting there trying to look blasé about being discovered out with another guy's girl.

"Yes," Olivia said, and then couldn't resist adding, "And here *you* are." She attempted to act as if Jennifer didn't exist, but that was made difficult, because David turned to her and pushed her forward to sit next to Red. Neither Red nor Jennifer looked happy with the arrangement. Olivia was sorry she hadn't sat next to Red. Then David might be the one looking unhappy.

"I called your home and your mother said you'd gone out, but she didn't know where. She acted like it was a federal crime for you not to have told her where you could be reached." David grinned at Olivia, attempting to make the comment about her mother seem like a private joke. He wasn't ignorant of the troubles Olivia had with her overprotective mother.

His one-dimpled grin failed to soften her. All Olivia did was nod and mumble, "Yeah."

She wasn't going to give him the satisfaction of being asked why he was there and what he wanted from her. If *he* could be out with someone else, then why couldn't she? She didn't owe him any kind of an explanation whatsoever.

There was a small silence during which everyone sat there staring at anything and anybody except each other, then Jennifer stirred and said, "Duffy, could I have a Coke?"

Red joked, "Ah, a lady who knows her own mind," and smiled at Olivia, but his attempt at easing the tension fell flat. Olivia's return smile was strained.

"Sure," David said and rose, heading for the counter.

Olivia watched him go, seething to herself but trying to appear as cool as an ice cube on the outside.

She had her act pretty well polished by the time David came back, but his first words ruined it completely.

"So," he said setting the Coke and his own lemon-lime down on the table before sliding next to Olivia. "Jennifer and I have been working on a big scoop this week. I couldn't believe this story came along right after she started working with me. It. . . ." He began to explain about the sports hero with one hand missing who was playing basketball for a neighboring town's high school, but Olivia had difficulty paying attention. Jennifer kept putting in her two cents, and every time she spoke she'd look straight at Duffy, as if the conversation were only between them. Olivia did not like the feeling of being deliberately excluded, and wondered if David even noticed what Jennifer was attempting to do. He didn't appear to.

91

David rambled on while Olivia fumed. How could this creep come in here and yak about the adventures he'd been sharing with that Jennifer person for the past few days while she'd been expected to sit around waiting for him to be able to spare her some time? Didn't he even have a clue as to how that made her feel? Ever since last Friday night he and Jennifer had been like bosom buddies. Olivia felt like pummeling him. Instead she sat there, outwardly the image of control, but inwardly boiling over.

Finally she'd had enough. She looked at Red, but he didn't seem to be having a better time than she was. So why were they there? Who was *making* them sit and listen to Jennifer and David's little dissertation? No one.

"Oh, Red," she spoke suddenly. "I forgot, I have to get home soon. There's that chore my mother wanted me to do. That's probably why she wasn't too happy about not knowing where I am." She smiled at him as if they'd already discussed this and hoped he'd play along.

He wasn't exactly speedy in responding, but finally, after she aimed a small kick at his shin, he said, "Oh, yeah. Sure. Let's get this show on the road." And he turned to Jennifer, saying, "Excuse me."

Looking vaguely dumbfounded, Jennifer slid out of the booth to allow Red to get out. David stopped talking, his mouth slightly open.

"Excuse me, David," Olivia said sweetly. She looked at him pointedly.

He swallowed, then slid out of the booth.

"But . . . uh . . . I could give you a lift," he said, sounding perplexed.

With that raven-haired fiend sitting between us — if not physically, at least figuratively? No way!

"No, thank you, David. I came with Red; I'll leave with him." Just like you came with Jennifer and you can leave with her! Olivia's manner and tone belied how angry she was. Slipping past David, she smiled at him, putting all her acting abilities to work, and took Red's arm, allowing him to guide her from Benny's.

Once they were in the car, Red turned to her and asked, "Is it really true? Do you need to get home?"

She didn't want to lie, but she really didn't want to be out anymore, either. Sighing, she said, "Sort of. If you don't mind." It wasn't exactly a lie, but it wasn't the perfect truth, either. How did you tell a boy the only reason you'd agreed to go out with him in the first place was to make another jealous, and now you felt as if you were a rag doll from which someone had pulled all the stuffing?

"Okay," Red said, sounding disappointed.

Olivia rode in silence while he took her home. At her house she turned to him and said, "Thanks, Red. I'll see you tomorrow," and before he could say anything, she pushed open her door and got out.

She didn't hear the sound of his car driving away until she closed the front door. Guilt stabbed at her for the game she'd been playing, and how confused, and possibly even hurt, Red must be right now. It had been a rotten thing to do, going out with him for the wrong reason. Red was too nice a guy to be used as a decoy. Yet it looked as if David's interest was being taken away from her, so what was she supposed to do about it?

Olivia remembered only too well how Walt had gotten infatuated with Jessica at cheerleader tryouts last year. If he'd been able to even *look* at another girl with that much interest, it was obviously a sign that he was ready to move on. And he had.

But not again! Olivia resolved. I will not stand idly by and let another boy drift away. Even if cutting the relationship off first is going to kill me, I will not be the one to get *dumped*.

CHAPTER

12

Tara Armstrong felt more and more like a fugitive from the law. All day long she'd been hiding: ducking into the bathroom — so often people probably thought she was ill — and making quick about-faces whenever she spotted Nick Stewart down the hall. She'd even skipped lunch for fear of his seeing her in the cafeteria. How long can I keep this up? she wondered, staring into the mirror in the girls' room. She was pretending to be trying to get a lash out of her eye. Now that she'd been in the john so long, girls were sending her strange looks, and she knew she had to have some sort of an excuse for dallying in there. But eventually even that wouldn't work, and she'd have to leave. Lunchtime would be over in about ten minutes, and she had to run the gamut of the halls to English, where she was expected to take a quiz. How on earth was she ever going to be able to even concentrate, let alone pass the thing?

Oh, Nick Stewart, why did you have to be a teacher? Why couldn't you have been the college student I thought you were at first? It would have been so much simpler. In fact, there was prestige in having a boyfriend in college. But instead of being able to hold her head up proudly at knowing Nick, she had to hide like a criminal. While other girls were going out to public places with their guys, here she was hiding from hers. Well, he wasn't *hers* exactly, much as she wanted him to be. But she was sure he'd call. If there was one thing Tara was a good judge of, it was whether a guy was interested in her or not. And there was no doubt about it — Nick was interested in her.

The bell rang. Oh, no, she thought in dread, it's time to run. Literally! By the end of school today, when she'd be expected to participate in cheerleading practice, she'd be too worn out to do anything but yell weakly. And what if today was the fateful day when Nick walked by the gym and glanced in? I can't stand this! she thought, charging down the hall.

"Late again, Tara?" some guy joked as she flashed by. "I thought you cheerleaders were supposed to be setting the example for us lowlifes," he called after her. Normally she would have shot back a retort, but at the moment she was severely lacking in humor. If I just get through today, somehow, someway, I'll try to do something good, she thought.

* * *

"All r–i–g–h–t, Sean!" Tara yelled, and the rest of the squad stomped their feet and whistled or shouted out assorted words of praise.

Sean stood there, feeling quite pleased with himself. He'd just performed an Arabian somersault to perfection. A great two-point landing, and his tuck with a half twist had been precise and clean. He grinned, took a bow, and then stepped aside so Peter could do his.

Peter stood there, psyching himself up, while Coach Engborg watched from the sidelines. She'd insisted on them using the crash mats, and Peter had the uncomfortable feeling he was going to be thankful she had. Watching Dubrow do his Arabian so crisply and perfectly had only increased the tension and anxiety Peter felt at performing the tricky maneuver. He glanced at Hope, expecting her to be watching him and ready to send him a thumbs-up sign showing her confidence in him.

But Hope was staring off into space, her expression slightly troubled. What was with her?

Not having Hope to give him moral support made Peter even more tense, and when Ardith Engborg gently coaxed, "Okay, Peter, let's go," he felt a premonition of failure.

Well, no more time to procrastinate. Four other cheerleaders were in line behind him to do the Arabians. With a fatalistic feeling inside, Peter launched himself forward.

He felt his feet lift off from the ground as he threw himself into the handspring, then, tucking his head and knees, he tried to do the half twist before landing on his feet. But even as he performed it, he knew he wasn't tight enough, and he landed flat on his back.

"Owww!" he groaned, writhing on the padded mat.

"Peter! Are you okay?" Jessica was the first one at his side, followed by the rest.

Six concerned faces peered down at him in a ring.

Smiling tightly in spite of his discomfort and embarrassment, Peter mumbled, "Yeah," rolled to his knees, then stood, angry with himself. And angry with Hope. What was the matter with her lately? She seemed to be off in space so much of the time — and not just at cheerleading practice like right now, but whenever they were together.

"You want to try it again?" The coach asked. She believed in getting right back on the horse that threw you.

"Yeah," Peter said tersely. He had the same philosophy.

Hope opened her mouth to disagree, but saw the look of determination on Peter's face, and promptly closed it. He knew best whether he should try right away or wait. If it had been her, she wasn't sure she'd try to do another somersault immediately, without time in between to catch her breath.

This time Peter's anger sent him through the manuever without a fall, the flip sharper, the half twist cleaner, and the landing solid.

"Much better," Ardith Engborg said, smiling. The squad clapped for him enthusiastically;

they knew what it took to come up from a fall and keep right on going with aplomb.

"Okay, Jessica," Mrs. Engborg directed, indicating she was next.

Jessica did the somersault, and as she came up from the familiar maneuver, the first person she saw gazing straight at her was Diana Tucker. Jessica knew Diana didn't normally attend so many of the squad's practice sessions. Why she'd suddenly found them so fascinating, Jessica couldn't begin to imagine. Maybe she was trying to get some pointers so when tryouts came, she'd have a good shot at getting on next year's squad.

Shrugging to herself, Jessica joined Peter and Sean on the risers to watch the other three do the Arabians.

Hope stood poised, arms extended in preparation for the flip. Her face was expressionless, but underneath its calm exterior there was rock solid determination. She was not about to blow doing this somersault, especially after what had happened to Peter. She glanced in his direction, and was brought up short. He was glowering at her! What was the matter with him? Maybe he wasn't glowering; maybe he was in pain. Well, she couldn't take time out to find out now; she had to do her somersault. Here goes nothing, she thought, feeling defeated. Feeling defeated seemed to be second nature to her lately.

She did the hand spring okay, and came up to do the tuck, curling herself into the tightest ball possible. But when she landed, one ankle turned painfully, dumping her on the mat.

"Oh!"

"This must be the day for spills," their coach said in a manner that was supposed to make light of the situation. She wasn't cold-blooded, but neither did she baby her squad. She knew the spill Hope had taken wasn't major; it was probably more embarrassing than physically painful. "It must be something in the ozone layer."

Tight, embarrassed laughter came from Hope as she tried to stand up. She tested her ankle, found it was okay, and walked slowly over to Peter.

"Are you okay?" Peter asked.

"Yeah." Hope's tone spoke volumes. She wondered why, when she'd taken the spill, he hadn't rushed over to her. The fact that he hadn't really disappointed her.

The four perched on the extreme edge of the riser watching tensely as the other two prepared to do the somersaults. Since two out of the first four to perform the maneuver had taken spills, it didn't look good for their chances of being given permission to use the new cheer at the next game.

But Tara and Olivia did the Arabian well — Olivia better than Tara, naturally, since for her they were almost automatic by now.

The four on the bench cheered and clapped.

Coach Engborg walked over to the squad as they stood waiting for her verdict. Today they had performed the Arabians so she could decide whether they were ready or not. And she had decided. They needed more practice. It was a decision she knew wouldn't be popular with the squad, but two falls were reason enough to put off performing the potentially dangerous maneuver in front of a crowd.

"I'm sorry, kids, but you need more work." She delivered the statement that came as no surprise, then added, "Sean, I'm assigning you to help Peter tighten up his tuck, and Olivia, I'd like you to assist Hope in her landings. Tara and Jessica, I want you to watch the other four in action, and try to assess where it is that Peter and Hope need help. I want to see what you both think." With that she strode over to the side of the gym to watch from a different vantage point.

CHAPTER

Dispiritedly Hope allowed Olivia to take her out to one of the mats and try to coach her, while Peter, looking thoroughly disgusted with the situation, followed Sean over to another mat.

Tara and Jessica sat there, watching for a couple of minutes.

Then Jessica heard someone come down to sit beside her, and glanced to her left. It was Diana Tucker. Almost absentmindedly, Tara got up and moved away. Diana hardly noticed.

"Goodness," Diana gushed. "Those things you guys are doing can be really dangerous, can't they?" Her comment seemed to be an idle one, not requiring any answer, so Jessica simply nodded and returned her attention to the four on the mats. Then Diana went on, "I guess to do them just right you really can't be thinking about anything else."

"Um, no," Jessica said vaguely, slightly irritated at Diana for rattling on.

"I know I sure wouldn't want to be thinking about anything else while *I* was trying to do that." She gave a short laugh, and added, "It would be as bad as thinking about something else while you were driving. You never know when you might get into an accident." This comment got no response, but Diana didn't expect one. She was simply laying the ground work. "Like last night, I almost got run over by a *garbage* truck. Can you imagine?" Suddenly Jessica tensed up; it was barely noticeable, but since Diana was watching her so keenly, she saw Jessica's hands clench and her lips tighten. "I didn't get a real good look at the driver, but at first I thought it was Patrick Henley. He does drive a garbage truck, doesn't he?" she inquired innocently, her blue eyes wide and guileless.

"Yes," Jessica said shortly. Her long, graceful body remained rigid as she strove to keep her attention riveted on the four working on the mats.

"But then I decided my mind must have been playing tricks on me, because some girl — not *you* — was sitting beside him, and she was hugging him. That's probably why the guy almost ran me down. How can a guy drive when he's being distracted like that?" Diana ended with a tinkling laugh and then exclaimed, "Gracious! Did you see that? Peter almost fell!"

Jessica had missed it. She was so busy imagining Patrick being hugged by Mary Ellen that she hadn't been concentrating on the squad.

Swallowing tightly, Jessica, said, "Excuse me, Diana, I have to go talk to Coach Engborg." And rising, she walked stiffly over to the coach, her mind in a turmoil.

What was Patrick up to? Why was he with Mary Ellen so often lately? Were they getting back together? And was Patrick trying to do it without Jessica knowing? Well, he'd *failed*. She knew, and it was driving her crazy. Jessica just hoped she'd be able to keep herself together until after practice. Because Diana was right: One needed total concentration to perform the Arabians without incident. Jessica was just relieved her coach didn't expect her to do more of them.

Ardith Engborg saw Jessica nearing her and made a quick decision.

"Jessica," she began as the girl arrived at her side, "what do you think? Where do Hope and Peter need work?"

Jessica thought, her expression pensive, and answered, "Well, it seems to me that Hope and Peter have the same problem. They're coming out of the tuck too late, and that makes it almost impossible to land right."

"I knew you'd see the same thing I did," Coach Engborg said with approval. "I want you to go out there and show them how to do the Arabian somersault once more. You really do them so well." She smiled at Jessica, but when the girl didn't appear to be in the least bit pleased by the compliment, the coach's smile changed to a frown.

104

"Okay, Coach Engborg," Jessica said, feeling unaccustomed terror. Not now! Don't make me do those things now when my whole life is going down the tubes and the boy I love is two-timing me!

"Jessica?" Ardith Engborg said a bit sharply. What was the matter with her? "You don't have a problem with that, do you? You're not afraid of performing them, surely. Why, you and Olivia have been doing them for weeks." She studied Jessica, watching the emotions flashing across the girl's face. She was just about to decide against making Jessica demonstrate the jump again when Jessica agreed, although she sounded resigned rather than enthusiastic.

"Sure, Mrs. Engborg, I'll do it." Why not? There were a lot worse ways to maim oneself, she thought darkly.

Trying not to think about what she was doing, Jessica trotted out to the exercise mat Olivia and Hope were on, and explained how Coach Engborg wanted her to perform the maneuver for the benefit of the two who needed a little extra help.

"Okay," Olivia said, unaware of Jessica's inner turmoil. "I know you'll do a great job. I'll stand by Hope and show her where she's having problems."

Peter, Sean, Olivia, Hope, and Tara stood off to the side and prepared to watch Jessica fly through the flip with her usual panache.

But Jessica stood there, her normally bright emerald eyes looking as if they were glazed.

Patrick and Mary Ellen, tooling around town

together in his garbage truck — it was hard to miss something that big! — for all the world to see. Especially Diana Tucker, who couldn't keep quiet about it. Oh, no! She had to come running to Jessica and tell all. Whether Diana had done it deliberately didn't matter. The damage was done. Maybe Diana wasn't positive it was Patrick driving that truck, but Jessica had no such doubts. She'd seen them for herself.

Patrick. And Mary Ellen.

Ohhh! She was so angry, her fists clenched.

"Jessica!" Ardith Engborg barked.

Jolted back to reality, Jessica began running toward the exercise mat. *Arabians*. She'd been doing them for weeks. They were a snap.

Except today.

Jessica flew through the air. Her right hand, instead of connecting with the mat, slipped off it, and Jessica fell, landing with a wicked-sounding crack right on her spine!

Horrified gasps escaped from six throats as the other cheerleaders and their coach witnessed Jessica's awful spill. Then all six, as well as some of the spectators in the stands, raced over to Jessica's prone body.

"Oh, Jessica! Are you hurt?" Tara wailed.

Elbowing her to the side, Sean growled, "Of course she's hurt. You don't fall like that and come out all right. Where does it hurt the most?" he asked, his dark, concerned eyes gazing intently at Jessica.

She lay there, her own eyes tightly closed, thinking to herself, I am hurt, but the most injured part of my body is my *heart*. She tried to figure out if her back or legs were broken, but aside from an overall ache, she didn't appear to have any permanent damage. Gingerly, she sat up.

"Jessica, are you hurt?" Ardith Engborg asked, her face the picture of concern. Why hadn't she listened to her little inner voice that told her not to have the reluctant Jessica do the Arabian somersault?

"I guess I'll live," Jessica said bravely.

"Someone help her over to the bench," Ardith Engborg instructed briskly. "Jessica, I want you to just sit out the rest of practice today. And as soon as you get home, take a hot bath. You may very well have some bruises tomorrow." The coach was all business again because she felt that was the best way to deal with the incident. Otherwise the remaining members of the squad might start to feel so upset they couldn't function. And simply because one of their ranks was now temporarily out of commission didn't mean that the rest couldn't still put in some practice time.

Sean took Jessica's arm and helped her over to the risers, even though she really didn't need it. As they neared the bench, Sean noticed something odd. Diana Tucker was no longer in the gym. When had she left? Before or after Jessica had taken her spill?

Hope watched Sean escort Jessica to the side of the gym and then walk back. She knew she and Peter were expected to continue working on the somersault, but now she didn't feel up to it.

No doubt Mrs. Engborg wouldn't want to hear any wimpy excuses; she'd expect the rest of the team to act as professionals. The show must go on! Hope thought dryly.

Turning, she looked at Olivia, who was also watching Jessica, a worried expression on her face.

Olivia didn't like seeing anyone hurt performing cheerleading routines, and that tumble Jessica had taken wasn't exactly an insignificant one. She wondered if Jessica was really all right or was simply being brave for the benefit of the rest of the squad.

"Okay, kids. I know you're upset because Jessica was hurt, but you must keep working. You can do it. I have complete faith in you all." The coach delivered her pep talk and then walked over to the tape deck she had at the side of the gym. Turning on the machine, she added, "Here's some soothing music to accompany your work." It was a joke. One of the louder Bruce Springsteen songs blasted from the player and the squad members grinned and laughed. Ardith Engborg was trying to make them feel better, and there wasn't a cheerleader among them who didn't appreciate the effort.

"Okay, Coach," Olivia called. "We'll work until we all drop."

"No, not until you drop. Until you get it right," Ardith Engborg corrected with a smile.

The five cheerleaders began practicing the somersaults again, this time with Sean and Olivia spotting first Peter, then Hope, by turns so no one was ever allowed to try the maneuver without heavy support.

Diana stood just out of range of Jessica's vision, right next to the door to the gym. Immediately after Jessica had taken her tumble and all the kids had scurried to her side, Diana had sauntered as casually as possible over to the door, then ducked out as the verdict had come down. Nothing broken! How could that girl take a fall like that and *not* break something? She must be an exceptional athlete. So that would mean Diana would have to come up with some exceptional tidbit of information about Jessica's darling Patrick to *really* break her incredible concentration. Scowling, Diana left the school.

CHAPTER

14

Tara sat next to Jessica, making sure Jessica was between herself and the door opening to the gym from the hallway. That way if Nick should walk by and glance in, he wouldn't be able to see much of the person sitting next to Jessica. Neither said anything, which was fine with both of them since they were so lost in their own thoughts.

Tara watched Hope and Peter trying to master the Arabian somersault. Why she hadn't had any trouble with it was beyond her. With my mind two floors up in the ninth grade math classroom, I'm the one who should have taken the tumble, she thought.

Jessica stared out at the four cheerleaders sweating and working hard. I'm a good enough athlete that no matter what is happening in my personal life, I should have been able to perform that stupid jump just fine! Instead, I'm a basket case. With the frame of mind I'm in, I probably couldn't even do a straight somersault, never mind an Arabian one. Why had she allowed herself to fall in love? She'd known all along that it was more trouble than it was worth.

Patrick. And Mary Ellen. Their names taunted her from somewhere within her brain, and try as she might, she simply could not expel them.

The two girls sat there, side by side but in worlds of their own. Tara's smooth, lovely complexion was paler than normal, her dark eyes wide and troubled. Jessica's shoulder-length brown hair hung in disarray on either side of her expressionless face as her tortured green eyes focused on inner thoughts. Neither was able to concentrate on the rest of the squad attempting to master the difficult maneuvers out on the mats, and neither was aware of the other's torment. When practice finally ended, Tara and Jessica sprang to their feet and left the gym with unaccustomed speed — but for different reasons.

Tara was continuing her evasion tactics. There was no guarantee that Nick was still in the building, but she wasn't taking any chances.

Jessica wanted nothing more than to get home and into a tub of hot water.

Hope, Peter, Sean, and Olivia staggered out of the gym, exhausted but feeling pleased with themselves. With Sean's and Olivia's help, Peter and Hope could now perform the maneuver to Ardith Engborg's satisfaction. Which meant that as a squad, they could with only a little more practice, be ready to perform it at their away game at Kensington.

"Thanks, guys," Peter said gruffly, as they trooped down the stairs to the locker rooms. He wasn't ecstatic about being indebted to Sean for his aid, but he was aware that without it he might still be having trouble getting out of that tuck in time.

"No prob," Sean said easily. He was feeling pretty proud of himself. Not only to be able to perform that maneuver competently, but to be considered good enough for Ardith Engborg to have him help others do it was a real ego-booster. Not that he needed his ego boosted, he thought, a cocky grin on his handsome face.

Olivia saw the grin and it annoyed her. She realized the reason was that it so resembled David's self-satisfied grin — minus the dimple, of course. When David was feeling particularly pleased with himself, he grinned in the exact same manner. Despite the fact that Sean had good reason to be pleased with himself, thoughts of David prompted Olivia to snap, "Yeah, standing around *watching* two people sweat certainly *isn't* a problem, is it Sean?"

Three pairs of surprised eyes swiveled to look at her. She ducked her head and walked briskly down the remaining stairs, turning sharply into the girls' locker room. She was disgusted with herself for allowing her anger at David to make her snap at a squadmate — unfairly. But still, she was so eaten up with unhappiness that she couldn't seem to find it in herself to apologize.

Hope turned to Peter at the door and said, "I'll see you upstairs."

"Right," he said, and walked on to the boys' locker room.

We're like two casual acquaintainces saying good-bye after a chance meeting, she thought defeatedly. There was that feeling again! When would it stop? The answer to that was almost as depressing as the feeling itself. She had a terrible suspicion the gloom wasn't going to lift until something happened — maybe permanently — to change her relationship with Peter. But would it be for the good of the relationship — or the exact opposite?

Jessica came out of the school thirty minutes later to find, to her astonishment, that Patrick was waiting for her in his garbage truck. The very truck in which she'd seen Mary Ellen sitting the day before — hugging *her* guy! His loose, easy grin infuriated her. How could he act like everything was just wonderful, when she knew what he'd been up to?

Patrick jumped down from the truck and began walking over to meet her. She plodded toward him, trying to figure out what she was going to say to him. *Been hugged by any pretty models, lately?* No, that was too obvious. *How's your love life — the other one?* That was probably too obscure for someone as dense as Patrick. Because it was a sure thing that any guy who thought he could carry on two romances at the same time,

113

without one of the girls getting wind of it, had to be *dense*.

"Hello, beautiful! Need a lift?" Patrick greeted her cheerfully with his usual sexy grin.

Jessica wanted to wipe that grin right off his face. But she suddenly found she couldn't. A little inner voice was frantically whispering, Don't do something you might regret. What if everything Diana has been telling you, or that you've seen for yourself, isn't what it appears? What if everything is perfectly innocent and aboveboard? If it was, then Patrick would say something. She'd gone with him long enough to come to trust him. Don't throw away a relationship based on evidence that might not even be true, the little voice begged. Give him the benefit of the doubt. Go with him and see if he mentions Mary Ellen.

She looked at him, her retort dying on her lips. Yes, she'd trust him. This time.

Swallowing, she murmured, "Uh, yeah. Great."

Patrick's grin slipped a little at his cool reception from a girl who normally would have given him a hug and maybe a kiss. The kiss would depend on whether there were a lot of kids around to see it. But there was only Tara, racing to her car without saying her usual greeting, and Hope with Peter walking to his car, both looking unhappy somehow. Sean and Olivia were having some kind of heavy discussion on the steps to the school. What was with the squad? They must have had a grueling session today to get them so depressed-looking.

"Okay, gorgeous," he said, trying to bring a

smile to her lips. "Hop in and my steed will take you anywhere you want."

Something that might have been a smile crossed Jessica's face as she stepped up into the passenger seat of the garbage truck.

"I'm really sorry, Sean," Olivia said, and tried to explain to him why she was so upset. "You might say I'm mad at a certain sportswriter, and I let it make me nasty to someone who didn't deserve it. Am I forgiven?" she asked, smiling sheepishly up at him.

"Aw, sure, Olivia," Sean said graciously. "My hide's too thick to let some offhand remark pierce me." He grinned before adding, "And anytime you feel like getting mad at David via me, go ahead. I can take it."

Shaking her head at Sean's cockiness, Olivia said gratefully, "You're too much. But thanks for being such a good sport about it. It won't happen again." She turned and walked away, saying under her breath, "Because I'm going to murder David."

Sean gazed after her, a distracted expression on his face. He had definitely not been batting a thousand where girls were concerned lately. Even girls he wasn't dating weren't exactly treating him like Prince Charming. Debby Brown had turned out to be so shy and withdrawn, he had been defeated in his attempts to flirt as he was used to doing. He figured it was by mutual consent that they'd decided they weren't right for each other. So now he was without a girl, and he didn't like that very much. Shrugging philosophically, he unlocked his car and got in. Well, he didn't have much doubt that another likely lovely would come his way. All he had to do was wait.

Driving home, Tara thought to herself, This is ridiculous. School has become an endurance trial. How long can I keep this up without *cracking* up?

Olivia walked in her front door to find her mother standing in the hall, talking on the phone. Her mother's first words caught her attention. "Oh, she just walked in, I'll put her on." Holding the phone out to her daughter, Mrs. Evans said, "It's David."

Resisting the urge to simply hang up the phone, Olivia decided to see what he had to say for himself, *before* hanging up the phone.

"Hello," she said coolly into the mouthpiece.

"Hello," David parroted, then added in a joking manner, "Just hello? No, hello, hunk? Missed you?" He chuckled to himself, and when she didn't react, he took a deep breath and cut the chitchat. "Okay, why were you out with that carrot-top last night?"

Right for the jugular, she thought dryly. She wanted to retort, Why were *you* out with that ebony-haired witch? But that would be a sign of jealousy, and she wasn't about to let him think that was what she felt. Because it wasn't. It was indignation. Instead she asked sweetly, "Who?"

"You know," David said in an aggravated

voice. "That red-haired kid. The one who looks like he doesn't shave yet."

Now it was David who sounded jealous. Stifling a laugh, Olivia returned in a prim manner, "Oh, you don't mean Red Butler? That very nice guy — "

"Red Butler? You have to be kidding." David started laughing, and Olivia realized too late she'd set herself up for that. A newspaper writer wouldn't miss the sound-alike quality of Red's name. Why couldn't he have a name like Killer — something to inspire fear in David? But she realized it would take a lot more than a menacing name to scare David.

"Oh, shut up, David!" she snapped when he seemed to be possessed by one of the longest laughing fits he'd ever experienced.

"S-s-s-sorry," he hissed, his chuckles dying down slowly. "But I'll bet he gets a lot of ribbing." Then he abruptly changed the subject as if he'd discarded Red as someone not worth thinking about anymore. "Look, Jennifer and I have to cover a basketball game next Friday night, so I was wondering — "

Not again! He was preparing to cancel their Friday night date! That was it!

"Sorry, David, I forgot I have something . . . uh . . . going that night. I'll have to cancel." Before *you* do!

"Huh?" David actually sounded surprised. "But . . . uh . . . I thought maybe after I got off from the game and drove Jennifer home, I could — "

"Listen, David, sometime when you and Jennifer aren't covering something so crucial, give me a call. In the meantime, don't be surprised if I find someone else to fill my free time." And this time she did hang up. She glared at the phone. The nerve of that louse! How could he do this to her without apparently feeling in the least bit sorry?

The phone started ringing the minute she turned away, and knowing it was David, she let it ring unanswered.

Her mother stuck her head out of the kitchen and yelled, "Answer that, Olivia."

"Yes, Mother," she said, and picked the receiver up, replacing it immediately. Too bad, David, she said to herself. But I will *not* be the type of girl who sits around waiting for some guy.

CHAPTER

15

David Duffy stared at the phone on the wall, and counted to ten. Should he try to call Olivia again, or give her time to think he wasn't, and then do it, hoping she'd answer? What in the world had gotten into that girl lately? Deciding to give her cool-down time, he turned away and retraced his steps to the booth where he and Jennifer were having a soda. That story they'd turned in on the handicapped basketball player had really impressed Perkins, his boss at the *Tarenton Lighter*. A lot of the input had been Jennifer's, too. David was pretty astonished at the grasp she had on both the news angle and the sports angle. She'd make a good reporter — if she was willing to work hard and be tough. She claimed she'd have no problem. But, then, so far it seemed anything Jennifer Clark decided she wanted to do, she did. She reminded David of Olivia; both girls had the same amount of determination. It was one of the qualities he'd admired about Olivia from the first. His strong, angular face was set in a frown as he slid into the booth.

"Get her?" Jennifer asked, giving him a long look from beneath her lashes as she sipped her diet Coke.

"Yeah," he answered simply. He wasn't about to tell her how the conversation had really turned out.

"So, uh, you'll be traipsing back to Tarenton right after the game on Friday?" she persisted.

David shifted in his seat uncomfortably. His discomfort didn't escape her notice. She made it her job not to miss much where David Duffy was concerned. And it certainly hadn't escaped her that he was incredibly good-looking. Even if he wasn't useful to her as a means to get into newspaper writing, he was worth cultivating as a date. Who wouldn't want a tall, blond, blue-eyed guy to be seen with?

"No, um, I guess I got our plans mixed up." David's voice was uncharacteristically lackluster, tipping off Jennifer to the fact that things must have not gone so well with his little girl friend, which was just fine with her.

Jennifer hid a satisfied smile and said innocently, "Oh, well, then, if you're free . . . um, why don't we go for some pizza after the game Friday? I know this really cool place over in Garrison. As long as we're in town, we might as well enjoy ourselves."

She studied him covertly, pretending to be

drawing the last drop of soda out of her glass through her straw.

David fidgeted a moment, still frowning, and then squared his shoulders. "Sure, why not?"

I'll tell you why not, a little voice blasted at him from within. Because Livvy is your girl and — but then he remembered that she'd been out with old carrot-top last night and hadn't seemed to be in the least bit sorry. Nor did it sound like she was going to be completely loyal to him in the future. Was she trying to cool things with him? And was this her indirect way of telling him? She'd certainly resisted getting into a romantic relationship with him when they'd first met.

Glancing at Jennifer, David made a mental comparison. Jennifer never seemed to play games. What she wanted was clear, and she made no qualms about advertising it. She wanted to be a sports reporter. It was no pretense. And lately she'd been acting like she wanted to get into a more personal relationship with David. David had no reason to think that she wouldn't be totally honest about that, too. So what should he do about it? He shifted in his seat again, aggravated at both Olivia and himself. I'm not good at figuring out females, he thought disgustedly. He decided that not doing anything was probably the safe course at this point. The next time he talked to Olivia, he'd see what she was like and figure out his next move then. Meanwhile, he'd simply enjoy Jennifer's company, something that was incredibly easy to do.

*   *   *

Before turning to walk up the front steps to her house, Jessica watched Patrick's garbage truck move down the street. Her mouth was an irritated line. How could a guy act as if everything were perfectly normal, yet keep a secret like he had? How could he be that good an actor?

Flinging the door open with more energy than necessary, Jessica stalked into the house. Not once on the drive home had he mentioned seeing Mary Ellen. Why? Why? *Why?* The word echoed in her mind all the way up the stairs to her bedroom. Onc thing was for sure: If that creep didn't mention his seeing Mary Ellen before their date this coming weekend, she was going to cancel it. Throwing her books down on her desk with a crash, she resolved, "I am not going out with a liar!"

If each day is supposed to be composed of only 24 hours, Tara was thinking, why do mine seem to be eons long? It was Friday night, and she was sitting in her big, white brick Colonial house, staring glassy-eyed at the television. At practice that day, the entire squad had managed to perform the complicated Arabians within the framework of a cheerleading routine, a version of the "Show 'Em Your Bite!" cheer, and Ardith Engborg was enthusiastic about how their performance would go at Monday night's game. Tara had other worries about that game. It would be the first time Tarenton played since Nick started teaching there. Was he the type who'd want to attend, even though it was an away game? Probably, she thought morosely. He'd told her he was a fitness freak, working out on Nautilus equipment as often as he could and jogging every morning before breakfast. So he'd probably be the kind of guy who also liked to watch sporting events. More than likely he'd even consider it part of his duty as a new teacher to show interest in his school by supporting the athletic teams.

Sighing deeply, she used the remote control to shut off the set. She had no idea what had been on that little screen for the past thirty minutes, anyway. Her mother and father were at a cocktail party, Marie had gone out to do personal shopping, and Tara was alone in the house. She'd thought the TV might take her mind off her problems, but it hadn't. It had simply become a source of annoying background noise.

She stood and walked over to the double French doors leading to the pool area. The pool wasn't open yet, but she wished it was. Maybe doing a few laps in it for a while would take her mind off Nick. Then she had to laugh. Take her mind off Nick? Impossible. Thoughts of Nick filled every brain cell in her head!

She turned listlessly to go into the kitchen and see what there was for munchies, and then the phone started ringing — no doubt some frantic client wanting her father. Tara wished she didn't have to answer it, but it could be important.

She walked over to the cream-colored desk phone and picked it up.

"Armstrong residence," she answered automatically.

"Good, that's just what I wanted," a pleasant-sounding male voice responded.

Tara sucked in her breath. *Nick!*

"Is this Tara Armstrong?" his voice inquired.

Oh, why hadn't she given him a false phone number? Then he wouldn't have been able to get in touch with her, and her life would be simpler.

"Yes," she answered carefully.

"Great!" If possible he sounded even more pleased. "Just who I wanted to talk to. And who I'd like to see. How about it? Can I convince you to go out to dinner with me tomorrow night?"

Dinner! In a public place where they could be seen by somebody, maybe another teacher at school who knew Tara? No, don't do it, Tara, she counseled herself, while her traitorous lips asked, "Why, where to?" She sounded ridiculously coy. She must be ready for the funny farm.

"I asked someone at work and he recommended a real snazzy place over in Garrison. Said a lady of class would love it, and since you're a lady of class, I thought that sounded perfect." Nick's voice dipped as he said that last sentence, sounding incredibly appealing.

A lady of class? Was that how he thought of her? What on earth had given him that idea? Then she remembered how he'd found her shopping in the gourmet section of the grocery store and supposed that was how he'd made the mistake. Stifling a nervous laugh, she answered, "Sounds wonderful." *Also suicidal.*

"Terrific. I'll pick you up at seven. Just give me directions to your place."

Tara recited the directions, wondering what on earth she was going to tell her parents.

"Until tomorrow, gourmet lady," Nick teased.

"Uh, yes," she said, trying to sound like a lady of class, and no doubt failing miserably.

She hung up, thinking fatalistically, Well at least the house will fit his image. It was a good thing her father was a successful corporate lawyer who could afford a nice place.

But what was she going to tell her parents? Nick did look young enough to be the college guy she'd thought he was, so she guessed she could always tell them she "thought" he was one. She could tell them how they met, bumping into each other at the grocery store. Surely they wouldn't find fault with her dating a college guy who shopped for his own food. At least she hoped they wouldn't.

"I came to say good-bye," Mary Ellen said, smiling at Patrick. "Pres is taking me to the airport right now."

Pres Tilford stood right behind Mary Ellen, not looking too happy about something. Patrick thought he knew the reason for the look of displeasure, and understood it completely.

"Yeah? So you were just passing by and saw my truck and stopped to tell me, huh? Well, I appreciate it."

Mary Ellen looked around at the interior of The Pancake House where the three of them stood just inside the door. They'd caught Patrick just entering the establishment for an after-work meal before heading home.

"We've got a little extra time, Pres. Can we join Patrick for a bit and have something to drink together?"

"Sure," he said easily. It was impossible for him to refuse Mary Ellen anything. He was nuts about her. If anyone had told him last year, when they were both cheering on the Tarenton High Varsity Squad together, that this year they'd be in the midst of a hot romance, he would have laughed right in his face. It still bothered him a little that he was dating his best friend's old girl friend, but since Patrick now had Jessica, things between them had eased up. There had been a little stiffness in the beginning when he and Mary Ellen had first gotten things going, but Patrick insisted that the only girl for him now was Jessica. Jessica was dynamite, Pres conceded, but compared to Mary Ellen, in Pres's mind, at least, there was no contest.

The three of them headed for a booth by the window, and then Pres thought to go back out and close the windows of his car since it looked like it might rain.

Patrick looked at Mary Ellen, observing the distracted expression on her face. She's already thinking about New York City and has forgotten Tarenton, he thought a little sadly. Would she *ever* come back? Then, smiling to himself, he thought of Jessica. He was glad she was happy to live right here in the same town as he did and didn't even entertain ideas about ever leaving. Yes, sir, he was sure glad he had her. He hoped he never did anything to blow things with her, because he didn't want to lose her. Ever.

"Girls' night out," Olivia joked, as she rode in Jessica's mother's car. She had called Jessica about some school work, and when she'd found out Jessica wasn't doing anything with Patrick that night, she'd suggested the two of them go shopping. Oddly, Jessica had leaped at the suggestion. Olivia didn't know why Jessica found the idea so appealing, but for her part there was only one motivation for her not being home tonight. The last thing she'd be caught dead doing was sitting around the house. Not after David had told her he'd be busy for most of the night and couldn't squeeze her in until the end of it. No, she wanted to be able to tell him truthfully that she'd been out. He didn't need to know with whom.

"Yeah," Jessica answered in a dry tone. It wasn't her idea of perfect, but still she'd been very pleased that Olivia had sought out her company. The two girls, great gymnasts of the squad, sometimes felt the force of competition between them, and they hadn't always been what one could call close.

"So where do you want to go? The mall?" Jessica asked.

Olivia gave a short laugh. "Where else is there?" she retorted. "In this town there is exactly one really great place for shopping."

"Yeah, but can you imagine if we didn't have

that? We'd be stuck with all these tacky little shops right here on Main Street," Jessica said with a wave of her hand at the small stores they were passing. There were okay places to eat along here, she thought, but forget shopping for anything decent.

They were passing one of the eating establishments, The Pancake House, when the traffic light turned red, seemingly without warning.

With a squeal of tires, Jessica slammed on her brakes and actually had to turn into the restuarant's lot to avoid shooting through the intersection.

"Good grief!" Olivia exclaimed. "There must be something wrong with that light! It's good you were so quick. And it's great that you could be so cool about it!"

Jessica gave a short, nervous laugh. "Cool? Who's cool? I think my heart just stopped. I have to pull over and catch my breath. What is it with the traffic engineers in this town? They ought to — " And then anything more she'd been about to say was blasted right out of her head as she saw all the customers of The Pancake House gaping out the window at her. And among those customers were Mary Ellen and Patrick! They were sitting at a booth together.

"Oh!" Jessica ground out, and stomped on the accelerator, throwing Olivia backward in the seat. Furiously she drove out of the parking lot as fast as she could. In her rearview mirror she caught sight of Patrick racing out the front door, with Mary Ellen close on his heels. No doubt he'd been upset that Jessica had found him out — yet again! She was glad he'd missed getting to her. He'd probably have been full of lies about why he and Mary Ellen were in the restaurant together. And she wasn't going to listen when he did talk to her. It was obvious what he'd been up to. And it was also obvious what she was going to have to do about it.

CHAPTER

Tara had chosen her outfit for her Saturday night date carefully, trying to look older than she really was. A dark gray sheath with padded shoulders, and gray stockings and black patent leather heels. She surveyed herself in the mirror and thought the outfit was more like what someone would wear to a funeral than out to dinner. Quickly she replaced the dress with an emerald-green one, which had a cinch belt in black patent leather to match the shoes. Not bad. Maybe a strand of pearls? They would make her look older, she decided, and clasped the pearls, a gift from her grandmother, around her neck before turning to leave the room.

Grabbing up her purse, she descended the stairs and peeked around the corner into the living room. No one there. That meant her dad was still in his den, and her mother was probably in the family room. Great. Now if she could just get out of the house without them actually *seeing* Nick, so much the better.

She walked over to the sheer-curtained living room window and peered through. At the first sign of that little MG she was history, she thought grimly.

Time inched by, as it seemed to do these days, and then finally she saw the little sports car drive up. Before he could even get out of the car, she ran to the front door, calling, " 'Bye, Mom," loud enough to reach the family room but not the den. She sprinted out the front door, closing it quickly.

"Tara," Nick said, smiling widely. Was it her imagination, or did he look even more handsome tonight? It had to be the clothes. They made him seem even bigger and stronger. A suit of navy pinstriped wool, a pale blue shirt, and a patterned tie in navy, red, and white. Classy, that's what he was. And she? Well, she could hold her own based solely on looks. I just can't say anything stupid and adolescent tonight, she told herself. I have to impress this guy so much that he's as crazy about me as I am about him.

"It looks like you're ready, too," he continued as he took her arm and escorted her to the car. There was just the barest touch of humor in his voice. "How would you like to take in a movie afterward? I hear they have a great theater over in Garrison that shows old flicks, like Bogart. In fact, someone told me *Casablanca* is playing tonight."

Tara waited until they were both in the car before answering. A movie? *Casablanca*? Good grief! That was as old as her parents. Was that the type of thing he liked? She could just see someone like Sean Dubrow at a theater that showed old movies. She almost laughed at the idea. Then she thought of something else. There probably wouldn't be many kids her age there, so she could spend time with him without worrying about being seen by anyone who knew her. In fact, there couldn't be a safer place.

"Yes, I'd like that," she replied primly. Rearranging her dress, she smiled at him and her breath caught in her throat. He was so good-looking! It was a crime. Why, oh, why did he have to be a teacher?

"Great, then we're on our way," Nick said, his grin wide and easy.

Oh, Nick, she thought. Don't look so happy. You don't know about me — yet. Someday he would, she just knew it. And, oh, how she dreaded that day.

"Jessica, that boy has called four times today and twice last night. I don't know what the problem is between you two, but I wish — in fact, I demand — that you go to the phone this time and settle it." Daniel glowered at Jessica, who sat on the couch in the family room with an expression on her face that was totally unlike her — one of rebellion.

Clenching her teeth, she rose, knowing she had no choice. So far, she'd managed to make her mother tell Patrick she couldn't come to the phone, either by rushing into the bathroom the

132

minute she heard it ring, or by ducking outside and pretending she never heard anyone call her. But she guessed six times was a lot, especially to someone like her stepfather.

Walking with feet that felt like they were made of concrete, she went to the phone in the hall. She wished she had one in her bedroom. Then she could tell Patrick anything she wanted to, without fear of being heard by someone in the family. She knew no one would deliberately listen to her conversation, but it was impossible for them not to hear something as they passed from one room to another.

She raised the receiver to her ear, wishing she'd been able to think of something clever and cruel to say. But saying something clever and cruel didn't seem to be within her abilities. "Hello," she said icily.

"Jessica, what is the matter with you?" were his first words.

The nerve of that guy! Here she'd actually witnessed them having their little rendezvous and he had the audacity to ask what was the matter with *her*.

"What — what — " she spluttered, and then said, "You have a lot of nerve, Patrick Henley. Telling me for weeks that there's nothing going on anymore between you and Mary Ellen. And then in one week I find you together three times. And one of those times she actually had her arm around you! I know you can't deny it because Diana Tucker saw it, too."

"What!" Patrick exploded. "Mary Ellen? What

— oh, I get it," he said slowly, then firmly he added, "Now you listen. I'm on my way over to your house right now. Don't you *dare* go anywhere. I'm going to straighten out this whole stupid mess once and for all. Do you hear me, Jessica? I'm on my way. *Stay there!*" And before she could argue he'd hung up.

She stared at the phone in her hand, and then practically dropped it. *He* was going to straighten out the mess? Ha! That was a laugh! The very man who was *in* the mess was going to straighten it out. That was rich. She'd just like to see how he did it.

She stomped up the stairs to her room. If she knew him, he'd be here pretty soon, and when he came, she'd be ready for him. Yes sir, she thought grimly, I am not the type of girl who lets a guy fool her!

Tara gazed across the white linen-clad table at Nick. The candlelight had accented the angles of his face, making them sharper and stronger. His blue eyes were staring unblinkingly back at her. They played with their desserts. Neither had really wanted them, but the romantic setting was so nice, they'd ordered them so they could linger.

"This has been wonderful," Nick was saying. "I can't believe I found such a great girl my second night in town."

I can't believe you did, either, Tara thought to herself. Out loud she laughed and asked, "Do you really think so? It couldn't be the wine, could it?" she teased, referring to the wine he'd ordered but which so far she hadn't touched. If he noticed, he hadn't said anything. Perhaps he did think she was a teetotaler. Or maybe he thought she couldn't handle it. That would certainly be true. She could just imagine how she'd start to act if she had alcohol in her system. She'd probably turn into a blabbermouth and let the cat out of the bag about her being a student. Never had she wished so hard that she'd already graduated.

"It's definitely not the wine. I thought you were a knockout when I . . . uh . . . bumped into you at the market." He smiled, his eyes crinkling up attractively.

Tara leaned forward, gazing into his deep blue eyes. "Oh, Nick," she said, "That's nice to hear." She tried to appear modest, something she wasn't exactly adept at doing. She was fully aware that she was good-looking, but she wasn't sure she would go so far as considering herself a knockout.

Nick reached out and took her right hand with his left, and as he did so Tara noticed for the second time that he wore his watch on his right wrist.

"Nick, are you left-handed?" she asked the obvious.

"Yeah. In fact my nickname's Lefty, but you can call me anything, as long as you *call* me," he said in a low, suggestive voice.

Tara was totally unused to dealing with a guy with this much charm and experience. She just stared at him, unable to think of any kind of a response.

Then she was saved from any embarrassment

due to her silence as Nick glanced at his watch, smiled, and said, "Now it's my turn to play the March Hare. It's late; we have to leave if we're going to make that movie."

They rose, he paid the enormous bill, and they left, with his arm around her shoulder.

It stayed there all through the movie, and on the way home he kept looking at her until she was beginning to fear for her life if he didn't pay more attention to the road.

Then, when they reached her house and he pulled her close to kiss her good-night, she felt like she'd fallen down a giant chasm, and she'd never be able to get out.

Watching his car drive away, Tara refused to listen to the little voice inside that was saying, He's going to drop you like a hot potato when he finds out you're a student and he's a teacher in the same school. You are a fool!

But she was positive Nick liked her. She was sure of it. The way he'd kissed her good-night wasn't a simple emotionless peck on the cheek. It had conveyed to her real feelings inside, feelings that could be similar to hers, although she knew he couldn't possibly like her as much as she liked him. Like? No, the word wasn't strong enough. She loved Nick Stewart. And nothing was going to stop that. But, oh, how it hurt to even contemplate what was going to happen when Nick found out she was a student at Tarenton High. What am I going to do? she thought, biting her lip. How can I keep him from finding out?

She mounted the stairs quietly so no one would

hear her, and crept into her room, closing the door with extreme care. If it ever got out that the new ninth grade math teacher was dating a senior, Tara knew, beyond the shadow of a doubt, that Nick would be in big trouble.

Jessica looked up at Patrick's earnest face. "You mean, Pres and Mary Ellen are having a romance? That you were only taking her home after she'd been at the hospital all day? But that arm around you — what did that mean?"

Patrick looked as if he had no idea what she was talking about, and appeared to consider this for a moment, then said, "Oh, I know what you're talking about. She was just assuring me that the next time she's in town, I'd see her — " And then seeing the look this information brought to Jessica's face, he added quickly, "and that means in a *casual* way. Pres and Mary Ellen are tight, Jessica. She and I have nothing — read my lips: n–o–t–h–i–n–g — going anymore."

She gazed up at him, and knew he was telling the truth. She felt like such a fool! Especially after he'd told her how Pres had been at The Pancake House with the two of them, but at the time Jessica had seen them in the booth together, he'd been out in the parking lot rolling up his car windows. What an idiot she was!

"But you know what I think this means?" Patrick said, smiling down at her in a manner that made her heart skip a beat.

"W-what?"

"That you're crazy about me and you were

eaten up with jealousy," he said, smiling even wider and looking pretty pleased with himself.

"Why you — !" she started to object to his incredible ego, but Patrick grabbed her in a big bear hug and murmured, "And I'm sure glad that's the way you feel, because that's exactly the same way I feel about you. Now, what are we going to do about it?"

His dark, melting gaze caressed her, and Jessica sagged against him.

"Well," she began in a teasing vein, then sobered, "I guess we could start with this." And she kissed him hard, trying to tell him with a kiss that she was sorry to have been such a pain and to have thought Patrick capable of cheating on her. She knew it had been terribly unfair, and she knew she had a problem believing a guy could like her so much that nothing and no one could tear him away. But Patrick was that kind of guy, and he deserved better treatment. In the future, she resolved, I am going to stop getting so uptight every time Mary Ellen comes back to town. And I'm going to start right now to make Patrick glad I *do* care. With that, she took his hand, and pulled him toward the front door. They'd been in the family room where her mother and Daniel had considerately left them alone. "I think we ought to take a walk, get out of here, and maybe continue this — " she paused to kiss him " — until we get it right!"

"I couldn't agree with you more," Patrick said, smiling happily.

CHAPTER

O livia could not believe her eyes. What was David doing here? She watched him walk up the front steps and approach the door, raising his hand to knock. She debated with herself whether she wanted to even answer, but realized that if she didn't, her parents might hear David's knock. Grudgingly she went to open the door, subjecting David to a coolly appraising look.

"Hello, Livvy," he greeted her, looking uncomfortable. "May I come in and talk to you?"

She shrugged as if it didn't make any difference to her. Stepping back, she waved a hand vaguely in the direction of the living room and then led the way, with David right behind her.

Olivia took a chair, rather than the couch, thereby forcing David to sit anywhere but right next to her. A picture of calmness, she looked at him. Underneath that exterior, however, she was extremely uptight. Had this bum come to cut things off between them? Had Jennifer managed to win him away with her fawning looks and interest in sports reporting?

David looked at Olivia helplessly, torturing the bill of his latest hat, a sea captain's cap. It was a sign that he was nervous.

Good, thought Olivia, refusing to give in one bit.

He swallowed and began, "Um, I wanted to know what's the matter with you." He stared at her a second and when she didn't immediately answer, he added, "What's the matter between us?"

There's the little *matter* of a black-haired witch, she wanted to say, but since that would give him the impression she was really hurt by all the attention David had been lavishing on the girl, she decided against saying anything about her. Instead, she played dumb. "What do you mean, David?"

Her using his first name instead of his nickname told him she was really upset with him. "All right, Olivia," he said, with faint emphasis on her full name rather than *her* nickname, "What gives? You've been as warm as Antarctica lately. What is it? If you're trying to tell me you're not interested in me anymore, I wish you'd just be up front about it instead of trying to chill me out. I don't like playing games. So, am I right? Is that it? Have you decided you don't want to date me anymore? I really thought we had something great going, but if I'm wrong — "

By now Olivia's temper had reached the boiling point, and she leaped to her feet, exclaiming, "Games? You don't like games? Then what is it that you call spending all your time with some — some black-haired, moccasin-wearing girl who wants to be a reporter? Can't she learn about the craft from someone else? Does she have to spend every waking moment in your company? I'm beginning to think she doesn't care a bit about reporting; she just wants you!"

Oddly, David flinched at that and turned a pale shade of pink. Had she hit on something?

"You're right," David said slowly, "but in reverse. She was only interested in reporting, and not in me. But she made a big play for me, and then last night when we went to this pizza place, some guy who works for the Garrison paper came over to our table. Seems he's a friend of her older brother, and he asked her if she was still interested in getting a crack at reporting on high school sporting events for his paper. There was an opening. He was pretty sure she'd get the job if she could show some of her stuff to the editor. We've been working on a piece that she had a lot of input on, but as soon as this guy told her about the other paper, she acted like I never existed. She was hanging all over the guy the rest of the night, and then she even got a ride home with him. Told me she'd see me *sometime*."

David looked so uncomfortable having to make this admission. Olivia stared at him in shock. He hadn't been trying to cut things off with her. She'd read him all wrong. But he'd gotten the same cold shoulder treatment she'd thought *he* was giving *her*.

Impulsively she came over to David, who was sitting on the couch, and put her arm around him. "I'm sorry, David, I didn't mean to turn the chill on — Well, that's not true. I did, but that's only because I thought you were falling for Jennifer and were phasing me out of your life. And I'd gone through that already, with Walt. I wasn't about to do it again. Do you understand, now?"

She gazed at him, her dark eyes troubled.

"Yeah," he admitted. "I think I do. I'm sorry if you got that impression. And I did spend too much time with her. It's just that she was so enthusiastic about my work. She was always pumping my ego up, I guess. A guy finds that hard to resist." He accompanied this admission with a wide, one-dimpled grin.

Olivia exclaimed in mock disgust, "Ah! So that's where I failed. I haven't been stroking your *ego* enough." She laughed and David joined her in relief.

Then, looking deeply into each other's eyes, they decided that talking it out wasn't good enough. David leaned toward Olivia, she leaned toward him, and they found that kissing was a great way to heal the hurts and misunderstandings between them.

Kids were stamping their feet rhythmically on the Kensington side of the gymnasium. Tarenton High's fans, filling only about half of the risers on the visitor's side of the Kensington gym, were trying to compete, but with fewer feet to employ, they were being drowned out.

"We gotta get this crowd really moving," Sean told Olivia. He clapped his hands and stomped his feet in unison with the squad, and glanced up into the crowd.

"Yeah, but first we have to get ourselves psyched up as a *squad*," Olivia said, with a troubled glance in Tara Armstrong's direction. Ever since they'd dressed for the game and had ridden the bus over to Kensington after school that day, Tara had acted out of it. Olivia had never seen her like this, one colossal bundle of nerves. "Sean, is it only my imagination, or is Tara a basket case tonight?"

Sean glanced in Tara's direction, and frowned. She did seem a little uptight. She was clapping and stamping like the rest of them, but in a distracted manner. Her gaze kept sweeping over the crowd and darting toward the door where Tarenton fans, who'd come in cars rather than the buses, were still pouring into the gym. "Yeah," he agreed. "She seems really out in space. Want me to find out what's the matter?"

Olivia looked at him gratefully. "Could you? I have to talk to Coach Engborg about something, and maybe Tara will open up to you better."

Sean smiled at this, thinking it was probably the opposite, but he walked gamely toward Tara, clapping all the way.

"Tara!" he called as he neared her.

Tara jumped, her eyes widening in fright.

"Oh!" she gasped. Then, seeing it was only Sean, she took a deep breath and exclaimed, "What are you trying to do? Scare me to death?"

"Scare you to death? What — ?" Sean looked at her in confusion. "I wasn't trying to scare you. But I would like to know why you look like you're running scared. Care to tell all to Father Dubrow?"

His attempt at levity was lost on Tara. She simply shook her head no, and kept on clapping. But Sean noticed her gaze was still sweeping the place, as if she was searching for someone in particular.

Shrugging, he turned and retraced his steps back to Olivia. "Won't tell. I guess you'll have to try."

Olivia frowned, and said, "Well, it'll have to keep until halftime. Here come the teams."

The noise from the stands rose to a crescendo as both teams began streaming into the gym. The squad turned to face the court and shouted and clapped for each team member as they were introduced.

Both teams retired to the sidelines while the starting players prepared for the tip-off out on the court.

Tarenton got the ball!

"Y–e–a–h! Let's hear it for P.J.!" Olivia led the cheer for the Wolves' tallest player, who'd managed to out-jump Kensington Kings' tallest player and knock the ball toward a teammate.

The squad fanned out along the sidelines, screaming lustily for P. J. Thompson, as Joe

Vogel, the center, dribbled the ball furiously down the court.

Tara tried extremely hard to really give her cheering her all, but she was so on edge, wondering if Nick was in the stands without her knowing it, that it was difficult beyond measure. What if he was right up there in the crowd now, and was staring at her? What could he be thinking? And what would she do if he was?

Tarenton scored, and the fans in the stands rose to their feet in joy. The squad led a rousing rendition of "Send It Home," a cheer designed to inspire the team to make more baskets.

"Send it home,
for a score!
Like an arrow,
Let's have more!
Do it right,
Don't get uptight!
Let this be our
V–i–c–t–o–r–y night!"

Tara spun in place and prepared to do a C-jump — and saw somebody looking straight at her with a totally shocked expression. She stumbled and almost fell, but Sean caught her just in time to keep her from cracking her head on the maple floor beside the players' bench.

Nick Stewart! Oh, no! He *did* come to the game. And now he knew!

CHAPTER

"Are you all right, Tara?" Hope asked, helping Sean get Tara to the bottom riser, where the redhead collapsed.

No! I'm about to die! Tara thought, knowing she was being hysterical. Was there even a remote possibility that Nick was staring at her only because he thought she looked so much like that "woman" he'd been dating? Stop kidding yourself, she thought morosely. All he had to do was ask anyone sitting around him who that redheaded cheerleader was and he would know it would be too much of a coincidence that they were both named Tara Armstrong.

The rest of the squad gathered around her, as if protecting her from the view of the fans. It was impossible for a cheerleader to take a fall and not be seen by the hundreds of observant eyes in the gym.

"Tara, what happened?" Ardith Engborg

asked, pushing her way through Hope and Sean to her. Tara looked pale and was breathing heavily. "Are you ill?"

Now that would be an understatement, Tara thought, but she knew their coach was talking about physical illness. And although just thinking about Nick up there in the stands made her want to throw up, it didn't count. What was she going to do? How was she going to be able to cheer for the remainder of the game without falling apart?

"Tara?" her coach spoke again, more firmly. Tara looked like she was in a trance.

"N-no, Mrs. Engborg. I'll be o–okay." By the time I'm twenty years old!

Struggling to her feet, Tara tried to put on the appearance of being totally in command of her faculties, but she knew it was a sham. Somehow, some way, she was just going to have to act like the professional she knew the coach expected her to be, and get through this game.

Coach Engborg looked dubiously at Tara, then shook her head, saying, "Okay guys. Let's get back to cheering this team." She clapped her hands, and turned to check out the action on the court.

Five other pairs of eyes followed her lead, but the sixth, Tara's, furtively turned to look up into the stands. Nick was still there, but now his expression was totally blank. Had he decided he'd made a mistake in thinking she and the person he'd taken out the other night were one and the same? Oh, how she hoped that was it.

"Y—e—a—h!" Sean crowed, and turned to pick up Hope and twirl her around. It was an impulsive move, but he'd picked her up simply because she was the closest female.

Hope felt breathless and oddly affected by Sean's exuberant action. Tarenton had just won the game, 78–76. A close, *close* game with tension galore. And now Hope felt added tension from Sean's touch. That she could even be affected by a boy other than Peter made the dissatisfaction she'd been feeling lately escalate. Oh, why, *why* didn't she feel what she used to feel? Why did it seem that she and Peter were in a slump? What could she do about it? How could she bring the life back into their relationship?

Suddenly Peter was at her side, looking displeased with Sean. Was he jealous? If so, that was a sign that he still cared.

Peter *was* jealous. He was actually surprised that he felt that way since he'd been entertaining doubts about his relationship with Hope lately. But if he could still feel upset at what Sean had done to a girl — whom he must still think of as his — then maybe there was something worth saving in their romance. And if that was true, then he was going to work on it. Maybe that was all that was needed: for him to stop doubting and start working. After all, they'd been happy together. So why couldn't they be happy again? They had a lot of time invested in their relationship, and it was worth a shot to try to save it. If it turned out he was trying to accomplish something impossible, well — he'd wait and see.

"Twirl your own girl, Dubrow," he said mildly, but with an undeniable visual message to Sean to keep his hands off Hope — permanently!

"Hey, cool it," Sean laughed. He didn't take Peter seriously since he was sure Peter knew he had no designs on Hope. He turned away and walked over to Tara, who for the better part of the game had cheered like a zombie. No one had been able to crack her veneer of almost catatonic distraction. She hadn't opened up to Olivia during halftime, and the rest of the squad hadn't even known where to start. No one had a clue as to what was the matter with her, and now, as the fans began swarming down the risers at the end of the game, Tara was looking absolutely frantic. She grabbed up her pompon and seemed to be looking wildly around her, as if she really didn't know in which direction she was supposed to go.

"Tara, what *is* the matter?" Sean asked, his tone more angry than caring. He was tired of this. If she had a problem, he thought she ought to feel she could confide in the squad.

She looked up at him, but her eyes didn't really seem to be focused. "Uh . . . uh. . . ." She swallowed and turned, saw something that made her gasp, and then spun back to Sean. "Quick! Please don't ask questions; just *get me out of here!*" The last five words of her plea were said in a desperate tone of voice that invited no objections.

Grabbing her hand, Sean turned and began pulling her out of the gym. He pushed people aside, ignoring the comments made about his rudeness, and practically dragged Tara out of the building and onto the team bus. Finding a seat way in the back, he placed her next to the window, where he noticed she scrunched down as if she was afraid someone outside the bus would see her.

"Okay, I did what you wanted. Now you owe me an explanation," Sean said firmly.

Tara's dark gaze turned toward Sean, and then her face crumpled. "Oh, Sean, I don't think you'd understand."

"Oh, yeah? Try me." Sometimes he really didn't understand females. And then other times they seemed deceptively simple. Sean wasn't sure which was the case this time, but he was willing to give it a try.

"I—I—" Tara began before getting herself together and launching into an explanation all about Nick and how they met. She ended with how she was positive Nick had spotted her in tonight's game. "I don't know what I'm going to do."

Sean stared at Tara's tear-streaked face a moment. He'd turned his body so his shoulder shielded her from the view of the team and the rest of the squad that had been pouring onto the bus for the past ten minutes. He couldn't believe this tale. It was just plain crazy. Tara dating a teacher! Either she was looney, or in love. There couldn't be any other reasonable explanation for her actually going ahead with dating Nick after she'd learned that he was a teacher. Tara needed her head examined. But it was too late now, anyway. The guy had to have recognized her. How many girls were there who were knockouts like Tara, or who had that same mane of red hair? Yep, she'd gotten herself into a fine mess.

"Look," he began, and then realized he really didn't know what to say to her. He tried again. "Look, the worst that can happen is the guy's going to have to write you off." This brought fresh tears to Tara's eyes, and Sean berated himself. Nice going, Dubrow. You can't come up with something encouraging. No, you have to hit the lady over the head with the truth. But that's just what it was — the truth. And she was going to have to face it.

"In fact," he went on, "if he wants to remain a teacher at Tarenton, he's not going to have any other choice. You know that, I know that, and it's a fair bet he knows that. So, even though I know it'll be next to impossible, you're just going to have to walk away from this and look at it as a lesson you had to learn the hard way. So you made a mistake. We're all allowed a few in this life. Next time, try to fall in love with a great-looking guy your *own* age. Like me," he said with a cocky grin aimed at trying to ease the tension.

Tara scoffed at this. "Oh yeah! Dubrow — the moving target." Then she sighed, and sat back, gazing idly out the window as the bus began to move. "I know you're right," she said dully. "But I hate it! Oh, why do there have to be stupid rules like teachers can't date students. What's so bad about it?" She didn't expect an answer to that, and she didn't get one.

On the trip back to Tarenton, all Tara could think about was Nick, and wonder what he was going to do about discovering tonight that she was a Tarenton High student. Would he get in touch with her? Or should she just waltz right into his classroom tomorrow and have it all out? *I don't want to do anything. I want everything to be the way it was last Saturday,* she thought, a tortured sigh escaping her lips.

Sean heard the sigh, and found himself actually feeling sorry for Tara. *I know how she feels,* he thought, remembering that Garrison cheerleader he'd fallen for. That had been a stupid romance, and he'd gotten hurt. Well, he thought fatalistically, it looked like Tara was going to have to learn the same lesson he had. No guy would ever be willing to buck the establishment and put his job in jeopardy.

CHAPTER

Tara didn't have to wait until school the next day to find out what Nick was going to do about discovering she was a cheerleader — and therefore a student at Tarenton High. Although it was late by the time she got home after the game, within twenty minutes of her getting in the house, the phone rang and it was Nick.

"Tara, I'm going to ask you a question and I'd appreciate a truthful answer to it," he began, sounding somber.

"Yes," she said in an emotionless voice.

"Were you at home all night? Or were you out? And where were you if you were out?"

Tara sank back against the pillows on her bed, clutching the white princess phone to her body. Oh, Nick! I don't want to have to tell you because I know what you'll do, she thought, feeling an awful pain in her throat, signaling she was about to cry.

"I . . . I was out," she whispered, and then added almost inaudibly, "and I was — at a basketball game. I'm a cheerleader." The last word came out in an anguished whoosh of air.

And now it was out! And now Nick would break her heart!

There was the sound of harsh breath being expelled from Nick's end of the line before he said dully, "I was afraid of that. I thought my eyes were playing tricks on me. But finally I asked someone who that gorgeous little redheaded cheerleader was, and when he said you were Tara Armstrong, it was all I could do not to yell no!" He paused, as if he were gathering his thoughts. Then, he said slowly, "Tara, I have to see you . . . alone . . . tomorrow after school. Will you meet me someplace so we can talk about this? About what it means?"

"Yes." The one word was torn from her lips. She was pretty sure she knew what it meant — it meant that he was going to dump her. He had no other choice.

"Where do you suggest?" he asked.

Tara thought a minute, and then said, "How about The Pancake House. No one is there that time of day."

"Okay. You have anything after school?"

"Yeah, *cheerleading* practice," Tara said.

There was a snort of ironic laughter from Nick before he said, "Okay, then. When do you get out of that?"

"About six. I'll meet you at The Pancake House at six-thirty. I'll tell my folks I'm . . .

uh . . . going out with the kids for a Coke or something."

"Okay. Then I guess I'll see you tomorrow at six-thirty."

"Yes."

It was clear that it was time for the conversation to be closed, but neither seemed to know how to do it. Finally, Nick just sighed and said, "Good-bye, gourmet lady. See you tomorrow." The remark was made in a wry tone of voice, as if he realized now what a misnomer his pet name was for her.

"Yes," Tara whispered, before hanging up. Tomorrow. The romance that never even got a chance to get off the ground ends. Rolling over on her bed, Tara cried herself to sleep.

Tara and Nick were gazing across the table at each other. Fellow patrons of The Pancake House didn't exist. As far as they were concerned, there were only the two of them. They'd been talking for half an hour by now, and it had become pretty clear to them both that neither wanted to stop seeing each other. Nick claimed, despite Tara's fears, that her being a student and his being a teacher shouldn't make any difference.

"So we'll just have to make sure no one finds out. We'll go out of town for all our dates." He was trying to convince her that their relationship could continue, but it sounded as if it was doomed to being a clandestine affair. Tara wasn't sure she liked that idea. They'd be like two furtive criminals, meeting secretly. It was horrid! But what choice did they have? There were no other options.

"I don't know," she began, looking intently into his blue eyes.

"Why, Tara? Why didn't you tell me when we first met?" Nick suddenly exploded. "Why didn't you tell me you were a senior at Tarenton High? The way you were dressed that night, and the fact that you were buying gourmet food, made me think, wrongly, that you were older than you are. If you'd only told me. . . ." He ended helplessly, his hands tight balls of frustration on the table between them.

"Because I was sure you'd never give me a chance," Tara admitted candidly. "I—I guess I was wrong, but . . . oh, Nick — " She stopped again, realizing she was actually calling a teacher by his first name. But it was hopeless. He'd always be Nick to her. She'd never be able to call him Mr. Stewart.

"You know, there aren't that many years that separate us. If you were out of high school, our ages wouldn't mean a thing." Nick talked earnestly, as if he were a lawyer for a hopeless case and knew, even though he was going to lose, that he had to try, anyway.

Putting his hand across the table to capture one of Tara's fidgeting ones, Nick opened his mouth to say something more, when a shadow fell across the table. He turned to see who it was, and felt sick.

"Well, hello, Mr. Stewart," the woman who stood beside their table greeted him.

156

Tara looked up at the sound of the woman's voice and almost gasped. Quickly and furtively she withdrew her hand from Nick's, but it was probably too late. Mrs. Oetjen, the principal of Tarenton High School, had already seen. What the woman thought about it, Tara couldn't guess. She hoped Mrs. Oetjen simply thought he was trying to console Tara about something, teacher to student.

"Hello, Mrs. Oetjen," Nick said stiffly.

"I haven't seen you since you started last Monday, and I was wondering how you were doing." The principal looked at Nick, but she acted as if he wasn't the only one on her mind.

"Oh, well, I seem to be doing fine." Nick looked so ill at ease. Tara thought she was going to scream if that woman didn't leave — soon!

"Well, if you find you need to talk to me, remember I'm available to my *staff* at all times." Was it Tara's imagination, or had the woman deliberately accented the word *staff*, as if she was sending a message.

"Thanks." Nick continued to sit there, his smile wooden, until, finally, Mrs. Oetjen said, "Well, I'll see you from time to time, I expect." Her gaze shifted to Tara, as she added, "I'll see you in school, too, I suspect, Miss Armstrong." And with that, she turned and left the restaurant.

Nick expelled a long, angry-sounding breath. "Oh, great. You said kids didn't come here this time of day, but you neglected to say that school administrators come here all the time."

"I didn't know she liked the place," Tara defended herself hotly.

They stared at each other, looking angry, confused, and hopeless.

Then Nick said, "I hate this! We shouldn't be arguing with each other. It's us against the world," he said, smiling faintly.

"Yeah," Tara agreed, returning the smile stiffly.

They looked at each other for a long time, not saying anything, and then Nick said, "We might as well go. Your parents will think you're drinking a whole case of Coke."

"You're right," Tara said, laughing with difficulty. She was forced to admit it was time for her to be getting home.

They left the restaurant, got into their separate cars, and drove off in two different directions.

Tara wondered what Mrs. Oetjen had thought about finding the two of them together. Had she thought it was perfectly innocent? Or had she suspected something. What would a principal think about finding a teacher and a student out together — with the teacher's hand covering the student's? Tara hoped fervently that Mrs. Oetjen didn't think a thing about it.

CHAPTER

 20

When the phone rang in the Armstrong residence late that night, Tara almost hoped it was Nick — and was *afraid* it was Nick.

She grabbed up the princess phone beside her bed before her parents could respond, and prayed they hadn't picked up any extensions.

"Hello," she said in a voice that was almost a whisper.

"Hello," Nick said, and Tara's heart plunged. Was he having second thoughts?

"I figured you might find it interesting what your principal said to me just now on the phone." His delivery of this statement was deadpan, as if all emotion had drained from him. Tara knew how he felt. She'd been on the receiving end of one of Mrs. Oetjen's little talks herself once, and knew the woman could really do a job on you.

"What — what did she say?"

"She said it hadn't escaped her notice that we

were 'holding hands,' as she put it, and she wondered if I could give her a reasonable explanation why a new teacher and a student were doing that." He gave a short dry laugh, and went on. "Of course I couldn't think fast enough, and my hesitation told the woman all she needed to know. She then decided that she must have neglected to inform me at the interview for this job that under no circumstances were staff members to have 'romantic entanglements' with the students." Nick made this announcement in a voice that was full of repressed fury.

"And what did you tell her?" Tara asked, afraid of the answer. But now her fear was of a different kind than before.

"I said I didn't agree with that rule, when the student in question was such a mature young woman like you, but before I could go ahead and tell the woman I intended to continue seeing you, she said if I broke the rules, she would be forced to fire me."

Tara gasped. "Fire you! But—but you can't have that. Nick, this is your first job. You can't have it on your record that you got fired from the very first job you had!" She stood and began pacing around the room as far as the phone extension would let her. "Oh, Nick," she said, woefully. "This is awful. I never thought I'd get you into trouble like this."

"Yeah, well. . . ." Nick didn't seem able to think of anything further to say. Finally he just sighed deeply, and said, "Look, it's late and you're probably as tired as I am, so . . . I'll see you tomorrow. Get some rest." He said that last sentence as if he knew perfectly well neither of them would do it.

"Yeah," Tara said vaguely and hung up, her mind a whirl with thoughts of how terrible it was that Nick seemed determined to put his job in jeopardy simply so he could continue to date her.

She flung herself back into bed and stared at the darkness. Her eyes were damp with unshed tears. But she couldn't break down and cry; she had to think.

Oh, Nick, she thought, in anguish. Just when she'd finally found the most perfect guy around, he turned out to have one very major flaw: He was out of bounds. Off limits. A teacher. But he sounded like he was prepared to break the rules anyway, even though it would cost him his job. He just couldn't do that! Tara couldn't let him. She was the one who had to make him see reason. And no matter how hard or how long she thought, she could come up with only one way to do that.

Tara walked down the hall, not seeing or hearing the kids that flowed around her, laughing and dragging things from their lockers in preparation for leaving school. She felt like a robot someone had programmed for self-destruction. She just hoped she didn't destroy someone else in the process.

She approached the math wing and slowed her step as the halls continued to empty. It was imperative that there be no one left — if not in the building, then in this wing — except Nick.

Or, more appropriately, Mr. Stewart, ninth grade math teacher. No one must see Tara talking to him, especially not Mrs. Oetjen.

She waited until the last of the students had trickled from his classroom, and then peeked around the corner of the door to make sure it was empty. He was the only one in the room.

Hugging her books tightly to her chest, Tara took a deep steadying breath and entered the classroom. On her face was an expression she'd spent the morning in her room perfecting. It was the look of a carefree, and uncaring, teenager. She'd even made sure her clothes were that of a young teen: worn blue jeans rolled up at the ankles, white crew socks, white sneakers. A pale blue sweater that was huge. Her hair was drawn back into a ponytail at the base of her head. She'd even gone into the girls' room just now to wipe off some of her makeup. She was perfect for the part she was about to play. She just hoped she'd keep herself together until she was done.

"Hello, Mr. Stewart," she said breezily, as she entered the room.

Nick was standing at the blackboard, erasing equations and formulas. He turned sharply, frowning at her use of his last name, and then his eyes made a hasty, but thorough study of her appearance. The frown deepened.

"What — "

"I just came by to tell you to forget about me. You see, I . . . uh . . . didn't know how to tell you this last night, but . . . uh . . . I was beginning to realize what a mistake it had been for me to even date you in the first place. You know, you *are* old," she said, her heart wrenching at the way this statement made Nick flinch. Keep going, Tara! Don't stop now.

"So, I was going to tell you anyway, that . . . uh . . . it's been real fun and all, but I have to have a guy my age. I can't be holed up in musty old movie houses or fuddy-duddy restaurants out of town all the time. I want to have fun with kids my own age at the local hangouts. If I continue to go out with you, there goes my social life. So, uh . . . well . . . look — I hope you can find someone more *your* age who you can date. Meanwhile, it was sure interesting."

All during this little dramatization, she'd been watching Nick's face darken in anger, his fists ball up at his sides, and his jaw tighten. She'd begun to back up ever so slowly, so when she got to the end of the dialogue she was ready to bolt out the door. Had she been convincing?

Ending with a careless shrug, she said cruelly, "Well, it has certainly been educational dating a teacher. Quite the experiment. . . ." Then to her horror her voice failed her and she was reduced to clutching her books even tighter and turning to leave the room.

Nick's voice, low and angry, made her pause. "So, you're trying to tell me it was all a joke? You agreed to go out with me just for fun? I meant nothing to you but an *experiment*?" His voice had risen on that last word, and it was Tara's turn to flinch.

Valiantly, she struggled to keep a lid on her

emotions as she answered with words that were the biggest lie she'd ever told in her life. "Sure. And it was a blast!"

"Why didn't you tell me this last night?" Nick demanded.

"Oh, well, I was tired and all. I mean, you did wake me up. So I figured I could tell you today." Did she sound like an inconsiderate teenager? Would Nick believe her? It was so important that he did. She knew full well that if they continued to see each other, Mrs. Oetjen would somehow hear of it and he'd lose his very first teaching job.

Nick stood there, eyes as hard as granite, until he finally said dully, "So that's it. You played me for a dope! You — "

But Tara knew she couldn't endure one more minute of this; she had to get out of this room or she'd blow it. Looking as blasé as she could, she said, "Yeah, well, sorry. But look, I gotta get to cheerleading practice." And with that she whirled and ran from the room.

Once in the safety of the girls' room, Tara allowed heartrending sobs to escape as she leaned up against the wall. Not bothering to even wipe the tears away, she stared at the floor and wondered: Had she been convincing? Had he believed her? She was pretty sure she'd given an Oscar-winning performance. If she had to judge from the look she'd seen on Nick's face, she'd done a smashing job of convincing him. And how it had hurt to do that! But it was the only way. She could never have lived with herself if someone had lost his job because of her.

164

Well, Tara old girl, she thought ruefully, you sure can live with yourself now! And doesn't your clear conscience make you supremely happy! A fresh wave of sobs shook her body, and then she roused herself, knowing she had to get herself together and get down to cheerleading practice. As it was, Coach Engborg was going to be angry with her for being late.

She walked briskly down the hall toward the stairs.

Jessica stood just outside the door to the gym, waiting. She was expecting Patrick to come by and watch today. He was trying so hard to convince her she was the only one for him. He was such a dear.

"Hi," someone said, walking up from behind. It was Diana Tucker.

Grimacing, Jessica turned to give the girl a hard look.

Diana's step faltered slightly at the lack of greeting from Jessica, but since she didn't understand it, she chose to ignore it. She was about to lay her latest fabrication on the brown-haired girl, when the door down the hall swung open to admit Patrick Henley. Her blue eyes widened at the sight. She thought he had a garbage route today. She hadn't expected him to be around.

"Oh, here comes Patrick," Jessica exclaimed, smiling in delight. Then with deliberate emphasis, she added, "It's so nice to have a really *loyal* guy around. Too bad you haven't found one like him, Diana. Keep trying, though." And with that, she ran up to Patrick, and kissed him long and hard for Diana's benefit.

When they broke apart and Jessica turned around, she saw that Diana was gone. Smiling to herself, she walked beside Patrick into the gym.

Olivia was stretching her legs, trying to get limbered up. She watched Hope and Peter enter the gym, holding hands and talking. It was funny how, out of all the kids on the squad, they appeared to be the ones who experienced the least amount of difficulty in their romance. She wondered what their secret was. Then, shrugging, she flopped on her back and did some scissor kicks. Well, at least she and David had everything squared away now that Miss Jennifer Clark was a memory. And I don't intend to let anyone distract David again, she resolved, smiling in determination.

Sean raced toward the gym, knowing that the rest of the squad was already there and he was late. It couldn't be helped, though. If old man Spencer hadn't detained him after science class to explain why his experiment in lab hadn't worked, he could have been on time.

Puffing slightly, he rounded a corner and practically knocked Tara Armstrong to the floor.

"Oof! Hey, I'm sorry!" he apologized quickly, and caught her before she actually made contact with the hard floor.

Looking dazed, Tara stared at him. It was then that he noticed her eyes were all puffy. It didn't take a professional sleuth to know she'd been crying.

"What's the matter?" he asked with uncharacteristic gentleness.

Tara looked at him, and sighed heavily. "Nothing. And *everything*. Remind me never to fall in love with an older man again," she said, looking down the hall. "I just broke things off with Nick Stewart." She didn't elaborate, but Sean didn't need her to. Her expression said it all.

"Oh," he murmured, turning her and taking her arm to guide her to the gym. "Bad?"

"That's not the word for it."

"Well," he said after a moment, "anytime you need a young guy to escort you around, don't look any further than yours truly." He accompanied this with a motion that was supposed to look like he was tipping his hat.

Tara gave him a tiny smile. She understood that he was trying to make her feel better. Sean could be a really nice guy when he wanted to. Her smile widened, and she said in a happier-sounding voice, "Maybe I will, Dubrow. Maybe I will." Then she added with a look that was almost like the old flirtatious Tara, "But don't hold your breath!"

Sean pretended to punch her arm, and chased her into the gym.

Cheerleading, Tara thought. When it was all said and done, cheerleading was the only thing that would save her from total depression. She'd give herself over to it completely — until the *right* Mr. Perfect came along.

When you are truly in love, is there only one answer? Read Cheerleaders #30 SAYING YES.

Pass the word!

Order these NEW titles chosen with you in mind!

- ☐ 33556-1 **THE BET** by Ann Reit $2.25 U.S./$2.95 CAN.
- ☐ 40326-5 **BLIND DATE**
  by R.L. Stine $2.25 U.S./$2.95 CAN.
- ☐ 40116-5 **DISCONTINUED**
  by Julian F. Thompson $2.75 U.S./$3.50 CAN.
- ☐ 40251-X **DON'T CARE HIGH**
  by Gordon Korman $2.50 U.S./$3.50 CAN.
- ☐ 33551-0 **HAPPILY EVER AFTER**
  by Hila Colman $2.25 U.S./$2.95 CAN.
- ☐ 33579-0 **HIGH SCHOOL REUNION**
  by Carol Stanley $2.25 U.S./$2.95 CAN.
- ☐ 40292-7 **THE KARATE KID: PART II**
  by B.B. Hiller $2.50 U.S./$2.95 CAN.
- ☐ 40156-4 **SATURDAY NIGHT**
  by Caroline B. Cooney $2.50 U.S./$3.50 CAN.
- ☐ 33926-5 **SEVEN DAYS TO A BRAND-NEW ME**
  by Ellen Conford $2.25 U.S./$2.95 CAN.
- ☐ 32924-3 **THIS STRANGE NEW FEELING**
  by Julius Lester $2.25 U.S./$2.95 CAN.
- ☐ 32923-5 **TO BE A SLAVE**
  by Julius Lester $2.25 U.S./$2.95 CAN.
- ☐ 33637-1 **WEEKEND**
  by Christopher Pike $2.25 U.S./$2.95 CAN.

📖 **Scholastic Inc.**
  P.O. Box 7502, 2932 East McCarty Street, Jefferson City, MO 65102

Please send me the books I have checked above. I am
enclosing $_____ (please add $1.00 to cover shipping and
handling). Send check or money order—no cash or C.O.D.'s please.

Name_____

Address_____

City_____ State/Zip_____
Please allow four to six weeks for delivery. Offer good in U.S.A. only. Sorry, mail order not available to
residents of Canada.   POI861